Double or Nothing

Dennis Foon
AR B.L.: 4.4
Points: 6.0

UG

DOUBLE OR NOTHING

DOUBLE OR NOTHING

A novel by Dennis Foon

Annick Press Ltd.
Toronto • New York • Vancouver

Second printing, October 2002

Annick Press Ltd.

We acknowledge the support of the Canada Council for the Arts, the Ontario Arts Council, and the Government of Canada through the Book Publishing Industry Development Program (BPIDP) for our publishing activities.

Edited by Barbara Pulling
Copy edited by Elizabeth McLean
Cover photograph by Lorne Bridgman/Westside Studio
Cover design by Chris Deixon
Interior design by Tanya Lloyd/Spotlight Designs
Cover model: Matthew Paradiso

Cataloging in Publication Data
Double or nothing

ISBN 1-55037-627-6 (bound) ISBN 1-55037-626-8 (pbk.)

I. Title
PS8561.O62D68 2000 jC813'.54C99-932944-8
PZ7.F66DO 2000

The text in this book was typeset in Neuland and Giovanni.

Distributed in Canada by:
Firefly Books Ltd.
3680 Victoria Park Ave.
Willowdale, ON
M2H 3K1

Published in the U.S.A. by:
Annick Press (U.S.) Ltd.
Distributed in the U.S.A. by:
Firefly Books (U.S.) Inc.
P.O. Box 133, Ellicott Station
Buffalo, NY 14205

Printed and bound in Canada by Friesen Printers.

visit us at: **www.annickpress.com**

A **Teacher's Guide** is available that offers a program of classroom study based on this book. It is available for free at www.annickpress.com and click on "For Teachers".

For E., A. & R.

CHAPTER ONE

This classroom smells moldy, just like this whole school. Mold oozes from the walls. The teachers plaster their rooms with posters of dead writers and extinct animals to hide it, to no avail. The building's not that old, but the mold set in about fifteen seconds after they cut the ribbon and opened the doors. It's a scientific phenomenon. Schools make mold.

Those spores don't get on me, though. That fine green dust that covers people the instant they sit down, that turns them into nodding zombies, Teflons right off me. I'm immune because I'm awake. I'm awake because my life has spice. What's the spice? No big secret, really. Let me explain.

When some people sit, they just sit. No wonder they're bored. No wonder life seems like a never-ending story. Let's say we're sitting in the cafeteria, twiddling our thumbs or pushing slop back and forth across the plate. That is boredom. But say I add some spice. I bet you five bucks that the next person to walk through the door will be a girl. Some might say, screw you, I'm not risking my hard-earned cash, and go back to sliding the slop. But a wise person would reply, you're on, and all of a sudden, we're staring at that door. Like that portal becomes pure mystery and excitement. Who will walk through next? Boy or girl? Who will get the money? This is the buzz. This is the thing that brings the spark, a flame, some pleasure, to the otherwise dull, useless, boring thing some people call life.

My pal Bongo understands this. Bongo might look like a Guinea Pig, and his brainpower might be in the GP's arena, but he's a player. A loser, but a player. And, hey, I don't begrudge that at all. At least he plays. At least he's into shaking it up. He turns to me in English class. We're both dying. The crabtooth, Mr. Cheese, a.k.a. Belch Face, a.k.a. Fart Machine, a.k.a. Most Boring Human Turd on Earth, is droning on about Hamlet.

Now, I got nothing against Hamlet. He was cool. He saw ghosts and had duels and was a kill-or-be-killed kind of guy. I mean, Mel Gibson played him between *Lethal Weapon 1* and *Lethal Weapon 2*, so this play can't be all bad. But my teacher, the Human Cheese, he's murdering Shakespeare. Each word that dribbles out of his mouth is pure somnambulism, and people are dropping like flies. I'm not kidding. Every couple of minutes you hear a thud as somebody's head hits their desk, dead asleep. Mr. Cheese doesn't care, he's just babbling on and on. He takes the snoring as some kind of affirmation.

That's when Bongo turns to me and says, "Hey, Kip, I'm dying here, man." He's pale, Cheese has vampirized his life force—and something has got to be done.

I smile. "It's resurrection time, pal."

The tension on Bongo's face melts in pure relief. "You're the man, Kip, you're the man. What's the bet?" Bongo's so filled with anticipation, I can see a little drool forming at the corner of his mouth.

"I say the Cheese does a belch in the next twenty seconds."

Bongo grins. "Five bucks he doesn't."

I shake my head. Once a GP, always a GP. Here we are, being turned into granite by the dullest human being on earth, and Bongo proposes a five-dollar wager. I almost fall asleep at the proposal, it's so pathetic. But I try to remain respectful.

"No buzz in that. Ten."

Bongo then has the reflex reaction of the weak: he feels his wallet. Not like he opens it, just pats it, reminding himself of the contents or lack thereof. A worried look crosses his face as he mulls over the odds of beating me (slim to none) versus how much coin he requires to get through the week. I shrug.

"No problem, Bong, forget it. Go back to the land of the dead."

Bongo bristles at the insinuation that he is faint-hearted. He pulls out his wallet and lifts the secret flap that hides his special stash. Produces a ten-spot.

"I'm in."

Now we are happy. Now we have a reason to live. We both pull out our watches, push the little buttons that set up the stopwatch function, and Bongo counts down.

"Three, two, one—Go!" Bongo whispers, and we click simultaneously. Mr. Cheese, mopping his forehead with his handkerchief, babbles on.

"But when Hamlet pulls back the drapery to reveal the dead Polonius, he has little idea . . . "

Bongo leans in on me, hissing: "Fourteen, thirteen . . . "

" . . . of the terrible repercussions his bloody act will unleash," the Cheese continues. "So much destruction from one death, the death of an old, irrelevant man . . . "

Bongo's getting excited: time's running out for me. Me, I'm hearing what Cheese is saying for the first time. The educational power of a bet is extraordinary.

"Ten, nine, eight . . . " Bongo's grinning.

But I'm not worried, no fret here, because something amazing is happening. Ten seconds ago I was bored to tears, nodding off, half-dead from watching the most tedious person on the planet kill me with words. But now, miraculously, I'm watching a human being transform before my eyes. I'm an eyewitness to an incredible metamorphosis. Suddenly, Mr. Cheese is riveting.

At least for us, because THUNK. Another kid's head hits his desk. They're still with the *old* Mr. Cheese. For them, time and space haven't been reconfigured. For them, there is no spice.

Bongo, thrilled, goes on with the countdown: "Five, four . . . "

Will he, won't he, will he, won't he? Bongo, feeling his chops, touches his wallet, imagining the dollars he's about to win. Bad move.

Through it all, Mr. Cheese is oblivious. "But in Hamlet's world, the fragile chain of life is broken, and the life-links . . . "

Bongo is feeling triumphant. To him it's in the bag. He's already deciding on how to spend it. On burgers? A new CD?

He's chortling: "Three, two . . . "

Mr. Cheese: " . . . drop like . . . "

But wait! Mr. Cheese pauses. Feels something. And from deep in his intestines, invisible gases rise, rise, rise, and . . . he belches. Unmistakably.

" . . . flies."

Mr. Cheese wipes his sweaty forehead again. Most of the class is snoring, so they don't smell the delicious perfume of sausage and pickles. Bongo does. He's wilted like a crushed daisy. Feeling sorry for the poor guy, I generously offer him a way out of the blues—and a bit more excitement for us both. After all, there's still another fifteen minutes left in the Cheese Show.

"C'mon, Bongo, double or nothing," I benevolently offer.

"I don't got it."

I look at his sorrowful face and, filled with empathy for his condition, I try to make him see the light.

But I know he's buckling, he always does. What makes Bongo a loser? Why can't he escape the mold? Because he panics, he gets worried. He stops having fun. And that's what it's about, right? Fun.

"Think, Bongo: win and we're square."

Bongo, defeated, shakes his sorry, furry head.

"Lose and I'm down twenty. I fold."

Sullen, Bongo hands me a ten-dollar bill, which I press against my nose. It smells good.

CHAPTER TWO

When lunch comes, I amble over to our regular poker game in the cafeteria, a game I started up last year, within minutes of arriving at this Mecca of Snooze, Louis Pasteur High. The game takes place in the back corner, with potato chips standing in for quarters. The actual money changes hands later in the washroom, in order to avoid the wrath of the authorities. Their ban on wagers is pretty hypocritical considering that we don't eat the chips, which they sell, and any doctor will tell you greasy potato chips are a hell of a lot worse for you than a little recreational poker.

Little Mike is supposed to be playing, which is excellent news, because he has deep pockets and no brains. Whenever Little Mike has a good hand, he gets excited and runs his tongue against his braces. When his lips start to flap, you know he's got three of something. Once he got so pumped a rubber band popped off his braces. I was lucky twice that time: not only did it tip me to fold before Little Mike unveiled a straight flush, his saliva-soaked rubber band missed me and hit Bongo, who didn't even notice it stuck to his shirt.

So I'm disappointed when Ms. Kruschev, my history teacher,

nabs me before I can get to the table. Apart from a bad case of dandruff, Ms. Kruschev is easy to like, especially because she idolizes me ever since an essay I wrote for her won the city competition. She begs me to go to the library and do a Web search for her on Hitler's invasion of Russia in 1941, and I can't refuse because 1) she's my best hope to score a scholarship next year; 2) I'm a war strategy freak—it's wagering taken to the ultimate level; and 3) I can hunt down the latest football scores and win a few more bucks from Bongo.

Hitler, as it turns out, made the same mistake Napoleon did when *he* went into Russia. They both underestimated their opponent. Forgot how big Russia was, how cold it gets in winter, and how tough the people were. Instead of folding their hands early, they both stayed in too long and got seriously burned. These are the lessons of history. Ignore them at your peril.

It took me the rest of lunch and a half hour after school to finish the job for Ms. Kruschev, so I have to head straight to work. While I'm waiting for a bus downtown, I'm watching these stooges lined up at a cigarette shop to buy lottery tickets. I guess nobody told them their chances of getting hit by lightning are a hundred times better than getting the lucky number and winning the $15 million. Those odds are for suckers.

On the bus, I pass the Sony Store, where Bongo, Little Mike and a few other guys are watching the TVs, betting on the World Series. I wish I could be there, but I'll still collect my five bucks from Bongo tomorrow. I know how the game's gonna end, because I did my research. The players, the stadium's geometry, the turf. Sometimes I think betting on sports is too easy. There's no spice in it.

I get off the bus and am instantly swarmed by a flock of panhandlers, who I refuse with a smile. How they ended up hitting bottom like that is a mystery to me. But not a big enough mystery to want to bother figuring out.

I cut across the street to where a big goose is painted on a window. This is the little restaurant where I wait tables. The Golden Goose is owned by my Uncle Ralph, which is how I got the job, which includes serving booze, which I am underage to be doing. The Golden Goose is a relatively classy place. It's what they call a "white tablecloth" restaurant, though we don't change them after every serving, unless somebody spills red wine. Uncle Ralph's cutting down on the laundry bill.

Tonight the place is hopping. There's a happy group of real estate dudes chortling and chugging Chablis at thirty bucks a pop, a bunch of couples gazing at each other through candle-light, and a spread of regulars. Halfway through the night a meticulous middle-aged accountant named Mrs. McPitted shows up. I guess she doesn't have much of a life, 'cause she comes in here at least three nights a week and eats with her laptop. Sometimes I make bets with myself as to what Mrs. McPitted will order. The odds are usually 2–1 on the Chef's Choice, and 5–2 on the mixed wild greens and grilled porcini linguine. Tonight I notice she looks a little blue and hasn't touched her bread basket, so I figure she's in the dumps and will be eating light. I bet myself fifty bucks she'll just have soup and down a bottle of wine in hopes of improving her mood.

She looks up at me and notices I am smiling. I tell her it's a beautiful evening and launch into what the specials are. But she stops me.

"I know what I want tonight, Kip. I'll just have soup and a glass of wine." Now I have to think fast. Not only am I about to lose the bet with myself on a technicality, Uncle Ralph will not be pleased. He makes his profit on booze, with the two hundred percent markup and all.

I sigh, a disappointed gurgle in my throat. She gives me a puzzled look.

"Is something wrong, Kip?"

"I shouldn't say it."

"Oh, come on, you can tell me."

"It's just that we have a beautiful Beaujolais right now. But you know Beaujolais, it doesn't keep, can't be sold by the glass."

She smiles.

"Then I'll take a bottle. Problem solved."

"Excellent choice," I say to her, and pay myself fifty bucks for calling it on the nose.

Back in the kitchen, my Uncle Ralph comes bustling over. Now Uncle Ralph is a very special guy. He's like the father I never had. He always steps up to the plate for my mom and me when we need him, like coming up with the damage deposit on the duplex when we had to move last summer. And the rest of the time he stays out of my face. Mainly, he's good to me 'cause I'm his only nephew and he liked my dad, his little brother, a whole bunch.

"Kippy, Kippy, we got a problem," Uncle Ralph says, and his big belly's starting to sweat through his shirt, the way it always does on those odd occasions when he gets nervous, every fifteen or sixteen minutes.

"What's going on, Uncle Ralph?"

"Don't push the Beaujolais any more tonight, we're running low."

"I just sold a bottle," I wince.

"Ooph, ooph! I don't know if we got it, Kippy. Start moving the Côtes du Rhône."

"One thing you've taught me, Uncle, is how to judge good wine."

"You got a nose, Kippy, it runs in the family."

"Well, that crap tastes like dog piss."

"It's rare, it's delicious."

"You could take rust off a car with it," I say, and then I eye him: "Uncle, what kind of deal did you get?"

Uncle Ralph lets out that guilty-sounding, high-pitched giggle of his.

"Hee, hee, hee. I'll give you an extra two bucks for every bottle you sell."

And he shoves a bottle of the toxic Côtes du Rhône in my hand. I sigh and stroll back out to Mrs. McPitted, who's playing solitaire on the laptop. She lifts her head and I give her a conspiratorial, excited look.

"You're not going to believe it! We just got this on special order from our dealer in Paris. You have to try it."

She gets a gleeful expression on her face. I pour her some.

She rolls it around in her glass, eyes it, sniffs it, swallows it down. And gets this pinched, pained look.

"It has a strange taste, I can't place it . . . "

My eyes light up at her acumen. "You have an amazing palate. It's aged in oak barrels from the um . . . Dalmation Forest. Extremely rare."

She's intrigued. "Seriously? In oak?"

I nod solemnly. "We're only offering it to a few of our patrons. Those who can truly appreciate it."

Or stomach it, as the case may be. She smiles and has another sip. "This wine is growing on me."

I nod, trying not to break up. After all, that wine really *could* grow on her. I see Uncle Ralph give me the thumbs up. I bring out the soup and serve a few more tables, then Uncle Ralph waves me over.

"You go home now, you got school tomorrow."

"There's still customers sitting at the tables."

"Nobody ever got rich being diligent," Uncle Ralph says, and he starts counting cash into my hand. Forty, fifty, sixty, seventy bucks. Then he raises his eyebrow and asks, "How much you got in that college fund now, Kippy?"

"Pushing twelve thousand."

Uncle Ralph whistles and shakes his foot. Don't ask me why, it's a thing he has.

"Ooph, ooph, that's sweet! Your daddy'd be proud of us both, you going to university and me making sure you get there and don't end up a lying slob like yours truly. Now go home and get some sleep. Ooph!"

Uncle Ralph is a wonderful, thoughtful guy. Living with my mom and with a job like this, I can save for the U and still have money to burn.

But I fall victim to Gambler's Arithmetic. I lost twenty bucks on the last bet I made with myself: I figured I'd get just sixty bucks for the night, but Uncle Ralph ten-upped me by giving me seventy. If you count the ten-up, then I'm really only ten down, so I split the loss. I try to console myself with the fact that it's only an imaginary ten-spot.

The rationalization doesn't work, though, 'cause I hate losing. Even fictionally. You know what I mean.

I walk in the door of the ratty duplex my mom and I call home. It's slightly better than the moldy apartment we were in last year, before the landlord evicted us so his nephew could move in. This new neighborhood's a step up, since people here sometimes cut their grass in summer and shovel their walks in winter. The English teacher at my old school was a lot less moldy than Mr. Cheese, but the Louis Pasteur kids are willing to bet higher stakes, so overall I'm happy we got kicked out and landed here.

It's almost midnight and my mom is sitting at the kitchen table, reading, with her mint tea in one hand and her stomach medicine beside the other. Her eyes are all puffy. She's probably been sitting at that table since she got back from work two hours ago, plowing through some thick novel by some old dead guy. I don't know how she does it: work, read, work, read. She looks up from the book and says the exact same thing she's said to me four nights a week for the last two years.

"God, I hate you coming home so late, Kip."

And I reply with the exact same thing I've been saying back to her. "Work's work, Mom."

She shakes her head. Takes a good long look at me with those sad, dark eyes. That look always gives me a chill. Her eyes are really beautiful.

"If you don't study, you won't get into university anyway. It's a damn Catch-22."

Oh man. The train is on the track and will stop for no one. This isn't a conversation that depresses me, really. I feel too bad for her to be depressed. She's really smart, has read just about every book in the world, always wanted to be a social worker and was enroled to go back to school when my dad kicked, so she never got to use her brains. That makes her determined that I should use mine. But she doesn't need to worry, 'cause I do. I use my brainpower for reading and writing and arithmetic. Okay, the arithmetic is usually about calculating the odds, but I consider well-placed wagers a practical application of my educational experience.

"Mom, I study. My grades are cool."

She pinches her shoulder, the one that seizes up all the time. Then sighs and has another sip of her mint tea.

"You'd be better off if you could just concentrate on school. You shouldn't have to work. I wish my jobs paid half-decently."

Did you catch the plural? Jobs. She works a day shift at the supermarket and a night shift three times a week at a shelter for street people. Barely has time to sleep, and she still cooks and does the laundry. I try to pitch in, but she feels this overwhelming sense of responsibility for me. Like I'll fall through the cracks or something if she isn't a total primordial mother.

I give her shoulder a squeeze. It's very tight.

"Mom, everything is gonna be fine."

She pushes the hair off her shoulder and reaches into her purse. It's one of those woven leather things left over from her hippie days.

"Here's a couple bucks for your lunch tomorrow."

I back away. This is the last thing I want. "I don't need it, I've got money."

But now I've got her back up. And you don't want to mess with Gemma Breaker once she's determined about something. You'd think all the pot she must have smoked in her twenties would have loosened her up, but no chance. Flexible she is not.

"You save your money for university. Now take it. Go."

I take the two dollars and shove it in my pocket. Then she lifts an eyebrow.

"How much are you putting in your college fund this week?"

"Twenty."

"And I'm adding a hundred," she says.

I wince. She just won't quit, and I'm the one who's gonna have to live with the guilt when she's groaning in a wheelchair.

"It's no good, Mom. You're killing yourself for me."

"You sound just like your daddy."

I look at her incredulously. "He called you *Mom*?"

She laughs and gets up to go to bed. Which is good, because she needs her sleep and I need to cram for a chemistry test. But no matter how hard I study, I don't think it'll help me understand Mom's chemistry. She's been out on like two dates in the last five years, and both of the guys were completely brain dead. I wish she'd take up golf or sailing or tennis, do something where she could meet some nice rich guy to take care of her for the rest of her life. Even if the guy was ugly, at least she could relax. She deserves it. But instead of fun in the sun, all she gets is the worry thing. No wonder she's got an ulcer.

That's the real reason I only show her a small part of who I am. I mean, it's for her own protection, right?

CHAPTER THREE

Okay, here's Gambling Lesson Number One: Attitude, attitude, attitude. If you feel like a loser, you will lose. Bongo, whether he realizes it or not, assumes he can't win. That spells D.O.O.M.

See, winning's a state of mind. Stay open and clear and the magic happens. I don't care what it is, bingo, blackjack, poker—winners win. They do. And I am the living proof.

Lesson Number Two: Never get ahead of yourself. Don't start thinking about what will happen if you win or if you lose. Celebrate too early and you're out of the moment. *Worry* too early and you're out of the moment. Once you're out of the moment, you lose the buzz. And when you lose the buzz, you lose the bet. You gotta be Zen, right? I heard somewhere that Zen guys get hit with a stick across the head when they stop being in the moment. Bongo could probably use that. A big whack across the chops. Make a gambler out of him.

First time Bongo and me check out the VLTs, I'm not totally out of it. You know, we play dice, cards, bet on belches, whatever. Most I ever won is like fifty bucks, right? So when I hear Vlitzes have invaded the neighborhood, I am most intrigued, because I've been reading about them on the Web. VLT stands for Video Lottery Terminal. Basically, they're electronic slot machines. The great thing that happened where we live is, they started putting the VLTs everywhere. Bars, restaurants, hotels. Used to be, if you wanted to bet underage, you had to get your own thing going. But now anybody can use them.

Well, that's not exactly true, as Bongo so aptly points out to me when we go into Jimmy's Jo-Jo Burgers for a taste of the VLT special.

"We can't go in there, man, we're underage," he whines.

"Nothing to it, Bong. Relax," I tell him.

"Doesn't matter," Bongo cries. "We'll get nailed, we'll get busted, we'll get killed."

I give him a little slap across the face. Very Zen. It's like cold water dumped on his head. He straightens right up as I explain the rules of the road.

"Lose the neurosis, pal. We've got ID."

This intrigues my friend.

"ID? You scored some kind of ID? Lemme see."

"Here it is. The only kind that counts," I say. I hold up a twenty-dollar bill.

Bongo doesn't quite get it, but that's because he's a GP, and GPs are nervous creatures. He doesn't understand selective blindness. I do, because I've done my research on the Web. I know restaurant owners clear ten thousand bucks a year on each machine. Four machines, that's forty large each and every year into Jimmy's pocket without doing a thing. You don't make that kind of easy cash sweating over Jo-Jo Burgers.

So, you might ask, why would Jimmy the Greasy Spoon Owner jeopardize his golden goose by letting underagers like Bongo and me loose on the machines? The answer, in a word: GREED. Like anybody else, Jimmy wants more. If the VLTs aren't being played, no money goes into his pocket. My age might be wrong, but my money makes me right. Besides, it's not like Bongo and me look like babies. Jimmy could claim we looked legal and apologize to the heat for not asking for picture ID. Or something. Worst-case scenario is he gets a fine. Big deal. Greed wins.

So Bongo and me suss the action at the VLTs. Bongo's all let's go, let's go, let's go. But I'm not for jumping right in. I want to see how it works. What I see is that three of the four terminals have zombies sitting in front of them. One of the guys is some kind of construction worker, covered in mud. Next to him is a lady in a business suit who looks like she runs an office, and next to her is a postman, with his uniform on, the half-empty mailbag next to him.

What they all have in common is the glassy look on their faces and the hand movement. They're feeding in rolls of quarters, five, ten, twenty at a time. All three are operating on pure robot action. How can you win when you're not even like . . . there? That's when Bongo starts ragging on me.

"Stop looking, man, do it."

"Five seconds ago you were chicken to come in here. Now it's all Do It."

Bongo shrugs. "But now I'm here and there's no egg on me. So show me your stuff."

Never one to decline a challenge, I pull out one rather dull quarter.

"Okay, I'm ready," I say, "but I'm only betting twenty-five cents."

Bongo laughs, not believing me for a second. But it's the truth. I'm not gonna risk turning into one of those androids. One quarter is all I am putting down.

"Lose it, and you'll go till you get it back," Bongo smiles.

"Lose it, and I'm gone," I say, with a look so somber and serious Bongo's fat smile flies from his face. He stares intently as I put the quarter up to the slot. I'm feeling really focused, like I can see inside the machine, like I know its game and it can't defeat me.

I drop in the quarter and click click click RING. Three sevens and two nines come up on the screen.

Bongo's delighted. "Hey, full house, that's four credits. You just won a dollar. Double up."

"Of course," I reply, push the "double up" button and hit go. Bongo is impressed at the result.

"Aces. Double again."

Without hesitation I double it. And win. I double that, and win again. Double that, and score a flush. One more time, and I'm so good, Bongo's starting to get suspicious.

"Whoa! You've done this before. Tell me this is really the first time."

"I'm a total virgin," I tell him, and it's the truth, at least with machines. So now I'm up thirty-two bucks and Bongo is pushing me to double again. I don't hesitate. Bing!

"Up to sixty-four."

Bongo's gaping. "Unbelievable. You cashing out?"

I grin. "I just started." I push the button and Bongo's eyes get wide.

"You got it. A hundred and twenty-eight bucks. That's it, take your money, run."

I look at him, considering the advice. "I should, shouldn't I?"

I ponder the concept of quitting while you're ahead. My finger hovers over the button for an eternity. Bongo leans in so far he loses his balance and his head hits the machine. As soon as he looks up, I push.

There's this hesitation, this supernatural pause in the room. Time stops. Everybody in the place is frozen, in suspended animation, living statues.

Then—BING!

A weird, happy screech grinds out of Bongo's throat, like some strange bird you're glad you've never seen.

"Two hundred and fifty-six bucks! You just scored two hundred and fifty-six bucks off twenty-five cents!"

He's banging me on the back, he lifts me in a bear hug, he tries to give me a kiss. I cut him off with a poke in the eye. But he won't stop jumping around till I cash out and let him hold the pile of bills in his hand, let him smell it.

On the outside, I appear to be totally unruffled. Bear in mind that compared to Bongo, anybody is super cool. But believe me, it was a rush. Over two hundred and fifty bucks in five minutes! Beats working. I vlitzed the Vlitz!

Bongo thinks I'm some kind of genius, but I know I'm not. If I can do it, anybody can. Because you make your luck. *You* make it happen. I did, I do. And once you're on a roll, magic keeps coming into your life.

CHAPTER FOUR

On a night off, Bongo drags me to see a movie. Drags is the right word, because I don't really see the point of going to the things. I sit there with the lights off and my mind can't stop twitching, blasting a million miles an hour thinking of better things to do. Why do people go to movies, anyway? You're stuck there in the dark, parked on your butt, staring at pictures on a screen. Bongo says he likes the stories. But 10–1 the story's just made-up BS. And even if it's not, it still is, because what you're watching isn't real. The real-life story's been totally changed and butchered to make it fit into two hours with millionaire, face-lifted actors saying the lines.

I don't mind going to movies with Bongo, though, because at least then we can do stuff to make it interesting. And tonight, he comes up with some *major* stuff. We're in the lobby. Bongo buys an ice cream, and while he's plugging it in his mouth, he gets this grin on his vanilla-covered face and elbows me.

"See that girl over there?"

I look. She's standing by herself eating popcorn. I haven't seen her before. Long black hair, sweet face, everything else sweet too. She's wearing a big man's herringbone sports jacket that hangs perfect on her. And she's definitely there alone, not with a crowd or a friend or anything, so she must be the independent type. My type. Suddenly she looks up and catches me eyeing her. I start to look away, as if I haven't been looking, but she smiles and wags her finger. She caught me. I grin and shrug. She smiles and flips a piece of popcorn high in the air and catches it in her perfect mouth. I watch, fascinated. Bongo interrupts with a proposition.

"Five bucks if you . . . "

I give him the Look Aghast. I mean, who does he think he's talking to?

"Five bucks? What do you expect me to do for five bucks?"

Bongo thinks fast. He, as usual, hasn't got a plan. He knows he wants to bet something, and he thinks it should concern this babe, but the rest is make-it-up-as-you-go-along. So I let him squirm and scramble, and funnily enough, a wager that has a peculiarly Bongo-ish charm is proposed.

"Smell her shoe."

"Smell that girl's shoe for five dollars? Are we talking the outside or the inside?"

"Inside."

"Who knows where her feet have been? Ten bucks."

Bongo nods. "Make it so."

I stroll over to her as she dumps the last few kernels out of her popcorn bag. I see my angle. I'm ready to offer to buy her another bag—for a favor.

"I see you like to eat popcorn," I say, with a charming smile on my face. But she holds her empty bag out to me, saying, "Would you like some?"

And before my very eyes, her bag is suddenly filled up to the top with popcorn. I stare, amazed. It was empty and now it is full.

"Did I just see that? I mean, did you just do that?"

She smiles this really devilish smile and says: "Do what?"

"The magic thing," I say.

She stares at me, like she's reading my mind. "No such thing as magic. Just tricks."

She reaches over behind my ear, and suddenly I'm looking at a perfect red, red paper rose. She hands it to me. Now I have to admit she staggers me. She's incredible. Beautiful, brilliant and has an attitude that knocks me over. She doesn't just do magic. She is magic.

I've just met the most amazing girl I've ever met in my life, and what do I do? I remember what I'm doing there. Let no man say Kip Breaker reneged on a bet. I smile at her.

"That's good," I tell her. "That's really good. Bet you can't pull one out of your shoe."

A flash of anger crosses her angelic face.

"Bet? You want to bet?"

Yikes. She's too smart. She's already on to me. What did I do to tip my hand? I backpedal like the Roadrunner.

"Nononono, just a turn of phrase. Truly, just phrases turning."

She eyes me, studying my face. I go deadpan so as not to reveal my ulterior motives. Years of practice at the card table pay off. Whether it's with a girl or placing a bet, the pokerfaced mask works every time. I can see the suspicion, a dark cloud, lift from her. And the sun shines through. So I make my play.

"It just struck me, the question," I say to her. "These materializations you do are phenomenal. Can you pull a flower out of your shoe?"

The dark-eyed girl smiles and shrugs. She reaches down. I can feel Bongo's eyes burning a hole in my back as she takes her shoe off—and hands it to me. I look. Sure enough, inside is a flower. A paper rose. I gape at her.

"God, you're amazing," I say, and I'm not putting it on. She is. Amazing.

But she just frowns. With this girl, flattery gets you nowhere. In fact, it seems to put you back a notch. So, going for the money shot, I put my nose in the shoe and take a big whiff.

Behind me, I hear Bongo choking on his chocolate coating. I love roses. Real or paper, I love 'em all. Magic Girl takes back her shoe, pulls out the flower and puts it behind my ear.

"You should wear it like that. Might get you some dates."

Oh, she really knows how to hurt a guy. So I say, "Does that mean I'm out of luck?"

She shakes her head.

"No such thing as luck. Call me sometime."

And she turns and goes into the theater. Feeling an urgency I've rarely felt in my life, I yell after her: "What's your number?"

All she does is wave goodbye, and the door closes behind her. I rush after her, running down the aisle, searching. Some stupid Hollywood trailer about some stupid Hollywood love story is blasting on the screen. And here I am, at the beginning of a real one, and I can't find my Magic Girl. She's gone. I check every row, every seat. Nothing. She's vanished into nothingness. Zip.

A broken man, I head back into the lobby. Bongo, eating a Mars Bar, rushes up to me and hands me the ten I just won. I take it, but the victory is feeling pretty empty.

Bongo's still dazzled by my performance. "Who was that girl?"

Depressed, I can only shrug the shrug of a guy who's let his dream slip through his fingers. But then, as we're walking into the movie, I feel something against my neck. I reach behind my collar and pull out a card. There's a name and a number on it.

"Her name's Joey," I smile.

All of a sudden, I see the value of movies.

CHAPTER FIVE

The Spendathon Mall is one of our favorite hangouts. Not inside, where many of the best and brightest from my high school slum outside the Gap, hoping to meet their genetic equals. I'm talking outside, where the action is, Sundays right around midnight, in the mall's empty parking lot. It's a work night for my mom, and an off night for me and the dozens of other kindred spirits who flock to the Sunday Smasharama.

Bongo has discovered this group of very buzzed guys I call the 3-Highs. The 3-Highs are high-rollers, high school drop-outs and very, very high. They put stuff up their noses that could fuel jet aircraft. Manny, who has slicked-back hair and wears Versace and sunglasses in the rain, at night, is actually 4-High, because he's all of the above, plus he's the High One. Manny, though I would never say this to his face, is a dope dealer. Now normally I do not associate with low-lifes, and under no circumstances would I actually compromise my pure body chemistry with foreign matter.

This bothers Manny. It's a matter of principle. He's proud of his products and wants me to approve. So he carefully sets lines of powder on the hood of his new Mustang.

"Snort a line, Kip."

"No thanks," I reply.

"I will," says Bongo, diving toward the hood. Juggernaut, Manny's number-one torpedo, effortlessly spins the Bong away.

Manny continues. "I'm telling you, Kip, all of my goods are one hundred and ten percent pure."

"I don't get the math, Manny."

"I do," says Bongo, cautiously moving toward the dust again. Juggernaut grabs my friend's ear, holding him back.

"Kip, it's purer than pure. What I give you to sniff is better for you than medicine. You go to the drugstore, they sell you shit that kills. You seen the recalls. Babies getting deformed from doctors' subscriptions."

"You mean prescriptions."

"Yeah, whatever. With me, you get a pure high, a high that is good for you."

"I already have my high," I explain.

"No, you don't," Manny says. "There are buzzes and there are *buzzes*. You never had a *buzz*, so you don't know."

"I know," Bongo says, making another try for the drugs. This time Juggernaut steers him to a spot on the hood, a fresh white puddle of pigeon guano. Bongo tries to pull away, but Juggernaut pushes his nose in it. Bongo, valuing his life, doesn't struggle. When the Jug lets him go, Bongo puts on a show for Manny.

"Man, what a hit," he groans, bird dung dripping from his nose. Manny's amused and allows him a pinch of the real stuff.

Personally, I have nothing against Manny. He's a good dresser, has a great car and he's an excellent businessman. When he's busted with his gang and sent to the pen, I will definitely correspond with him, assuming he learns to write. But he'll never understand why drugs leave me flat. I don't need them. I already have my high. I'm here for the derby, a true gambler's delight. But that's merely the second reason I'm super-buzzed. The first is, I met Magic Girl! I can't get her face out of my head, which is a superbly wonderful thing, because I love thinking about her.

Donkey, a gigantic, goofy-looking guy who wears a huge red leather jacket, announces the derby is about to begin. Donkey is not just goofy-looking. He is also completely wacko. Rumor has it he had an athletic infancy. The story goes that his dad, who had just bombed in his tryout for the Winnipeg Blue Bombers, had a big wake for his football dreams that night. He and his buds were short a pigskin in a beer-crazed pickup game, so baby Donkey, bearing the closest resemblance to a football, was the last-minute replacement. The only reason Donkey survived the game was that they were all too drunk to finish playing. Donkey's dad's career in football may have ended that day, but Donkey had now, for all practical purposes, become a football. Which is why Manny likes having him around. He's loyal, big and pulverizes anybody who crosses Manny.

Donkey gets in his '87 Buick. Phil the Bill, a lanky, chain-smoking, tongue- and lip-pierced hothead, crawls into his Mazda. James Ripley, totally straight-looking, an all-A student and a complete maniac behind the wheel, jumps into his Jeep.

"Start your engines!" yells Manny. The motors roar. Bongo launches into the national anthem but Manny shoves an elbow in his mouth. "Bets are open!" Manny shouts over the din. And there's a mad rush to Juggernaut to place the bets.

I'm pumped. I fight through the crowd and put down twenty on Phil the Bill to win. He's fearless, mean and suicidal, all excellent attributes for the race. I guess it's not completely accurate to call this a race. It's more like a stop-action event. The action is, the drivers floor it and head straight for the concrete wall at the end of the parking lot. The stop part is when they hit the cement. The winner is the first guy who smashes into the wall. He gets a quarter of the kitty. The runner-up gets his insurance deductible paid, if he plays his cards right. And the rest of us get a great show and a chance to double our money.

"Goooo!" screams Manny, and they're off. Much to my dismay, James Ripley, in his four-wheel drive, is in front. I can't believe this. Phil the Bill is a total grease monkey. I know through impeccable sources that he installed a Porsche engine under the hood of that rusted-out Mazda two weeks ago and it can fly. But he's grounded tonight, it seems, and I'm about to drop twenty bucks.

Bongo, meanwhile, is chanting "Donkey, Donkey, Donkey," despite the fact that the Donk is trailing behind Ripley and my man. But it goes from bad to worse. The Mazda is losing speed, not gaining, and Donkey pulls into second. How can this be?

Then, all of a sudden, we hear this ear-shattering sound. A

kind of mystic roar. It's the Porsche engine kicking in, backfiring explosions. And then the Mazda goes! It blasts like a rocket, past the Donkey, past Ripley, and bullets right into the wall. Metal crunching, glass breaking . . . music to my ears.

There's a horrible squeal that makes everybody wince. Ripley, ever the straight man, bails. As he slams on his anti-lock brakes, his Jeep skids, burning brake pads and rubber, and spins, its rear bumpers kissing the concrete.

But Donkey, true to form, is no quitter. Opting for the deductible, he floors it to the wall. The Buick hits, and Donkey goes flying. Smashes through the windshield and bounces off the wall, landing on the hood. Seems he wasn't wearing his seatbelt.

Everybody freaks. We run to his car. Is he alive? Is he dead? This is the first casualty the event's ever had. After all, the drivers know what they're getting into, so they buckle up. I mean, wouldn't you?

Bongo charges over to Donkey, tears streaming down his face. He's always had a special thing for the human football. There's a terrible silence. We're all staring at this eighteen-year-old giant, covered in blood and glass, lying comatose on the hood. This is bad, couldn't be worse.

Then, all jaws drop. Donkey's eyes flutter open. He sits up. Everybody cheers. Dazed but apparently unharmed, Donkey smiles. "Did I win?"

Bongo's thrilled. Donkey's alive to try dying again another day. Bongo hugs the big tree stump, but Donkey's inconsolable, he can't believe he didn't win. His face still dripping blood, he jumps back behind the wheel. Stunned or in shock or something, he wants to smash into the wall again. And he would, too, except for the fact that his car is dead.

Later I ask Bongo what's this thing he's got for Donkey.

"I love him 'cause he's like you, Kip."

"Like me? Are you nuts?"

"He's fearless. Total cojones."

"No, he's not, he's got a damaged brain."

Bongo looks at me, mulling that over. Then he says, "Whatever."

I collect my forty bucks from Manny. Part One of my natural high is complete. Now it's on to Part Two. Magic Girl.

CHAPTER SIX

I get home after three, but Mom's still at work. She kills me, putting in seventy hours a week for peanuts. My dad did the same thing when the work came in. It's no wonder he packed it in so young. They're both excellent role models. What they've taught me is: Don't be like them. I'm not waking up one day to find myself broke and stuck working three jobs to make ends meet. Not me.

In the morning, the alarm breaks my head open and my eyes let in the light. I drag myself up. Mom's still asleep. Figuring this is as good a time as any, I pull out the card Joey gave me. I'm not trembling when I dial the number, I'm not even nervous. I'm just trying to decide on the best opening line.

I could do the dazzle thing, like right off the bat, before even saying hello, tell her I can't stop thinking about her. But her bullshit detector would blow me out of the water. I could start low-key with the small talk, nice and easy. In the end, I decide to just take it as it comes. Say hello and see what happens.

The phone rings once, twice, three times. I'm about to pack it in when somebody picks up: "Hello?" It sounds like her, but I can't be sure.

"Hi, Joey? This is Kip . . . "

Before I can say another word, the voice that I think is her says, "Come to the Playhouse tonight at eight o'clock. Your ticket will be at the box office. See you there."

CLICK, and I get a dial tone. Am I dreaming? Did I really hear what I just heard? Did she have it all planned? What if I was working tonight? Even if I was, though, I'd call in sick. I wouldn't miss this. Is she that sure of herself? Or was she just calling my bluff? I've been with more than a few girls, but Joey is like no other. She is one of a kind.

School passes by in a blur. It's like my body parts are all functioning independently. My mouth is effortlessly answering the teacher's questions: "Yes, Napoleon was first exiled to the island of Elba, Ms. Kruschev." My hand is writing "Joey" over and over again in my notebook. My ears are hearing some kind of music that I'm trying to remember. And then it hits me. She's meeting me at the Playhouse, the posh theater in town.

I have a memory of that place. I was like four, and I went with my mom and dad to some kind of concert. I was bored, kept kicking my feet, so my dad gave me his lighter to keep me occupied. Interesting choice of a toy for a four-year-old. I could see my face in it, could make the lights reflect off it. Then I lit it. The guy next to me started hitting the flame with his program, which nearly caught on fire. My dad grabbed the lighter, pulled me out of the concert. We sat in the lobby until the end, me on his lap clicking the lighter over and over again.

Suddenly I hear my mouth responding to another question. "After the Battle of Waterloo, Napoleon was exiled to the island of Saint Helena," it says to Ms. Kruschev. "He died there of stomach cancer in 1821."

Somehow my various body parts get me through the day. I don't know if anybody but me notices. I wonder if Napoleon had separately functioning body parts too.

At home, I sift through my clothes, trying to figure out what to wear. There's not a huge selection, actually. Blue jeans or black jeans. Blue shirt or black shirt. I want to go a bit formal, this being a special occasion and all, so I pick black on black. I evaluate myself in the mirror. What if she hates black? Seems doubtful, but I decide to hedge my bets and put on the blue shirt. I put my nose to the mirror and examine my eyes. They're clear, no blood vessels popping out. They actually look kind of tranquil, very yin-yang. My heart's pumping, you wouldn't believe how hard. I hold out my hands. They're steady. Check breath: sweet. I'm ready for the Magic Girl. I hope.

The huge illuminated sign outside the Playhouse reads KING HEWITT—MASTER ILLUSIONIST. I've heard of him. He's like the real thing. A big poster says he's been on talk shows, TV specials, you name it. He's an older guy, a local legend. Doesn't perform that much in town, though; probably too busy on the international circuit. Maybe Joey wanted to come here for our first date because she's a bit of a magician herself. But why the mystery?

I work my way through the crowd as people push toward the entrance doors. I'm not quite sure what I'm supposed to do, but when I cut over to the box office and give the guy my name, I get the ticket. I can't figure her out. The ticket's not cheap. And this theater's really classy, people walking around in suits and ties and furs. I feel like I should go home and change. And I almost would, except for the fact that there's zero time. I wait outside for a while looking for her, then I go in. Hang in the lobby, peering past the people, looking. I don't see her anywhere.

Then the bell starts to go and they're flicking the lights; the show's about to begin. I smack myself on the head. She must already be in the theater. I boot it down the aisle and bullet to Row 5. The row is packed, and there's only one empty seat. Mine. I squeeze through feet and knees to get to my place, then turn to the guy next to me.

"Are you sure you're in the right seat?"

He's an uptight business dude in a suit who doesn't appreciate the question. But I keep staring at him until he pulls out his ticket. I check it. He's in the right spot. I turn to the lady on my left. She's already holding her ticket for me to inspect. Sure enough, that's her seat.

So now I'm feeling miffed and stiffed. Some date. I get a free ticket, but she's a no-show. The magic's starting to fade from Magic Girl. Grumpy and peeved, I'm ready to bolt when the lights go down. I figure I'll watch the first half and peel at intermission.

Total darkness. Then a tiny flame of light, floating in the air. It explodes, and the entire stage is filled with fire. I can feel the heat from where I'm sitting. It's blistering. Then out of the hottest part of the fire steps King Hewitt. He's something. Bigger than life. Glittering silver suit. Long gray hair. The audience is giving him huge applause.

He waves his arm and the flames vanish. Snaps his fingers, and a big silver cube descends from the ceiling. He reaches up with his cane and opens a door in the front of the box. There's nothing inside. To demonstrate its complete emptiness, he pulls a flamethrower from the wings and blasts the interior with fire. He keeps throwing flame all around the suspended cube, proving that it is floating free in the air. The crowd is mesmerized. They love this guy.

He closes the door. And then the Master Illusionist speaks.

"An empty cube. Like man, an empty vessel. Pure emptiness. Like the human heart. Unless it's filled with love."

Then, with a wave of his cane, he flicks the door open. A girl dressed in a little sequined dress is sitting there. My jaw hits my chest.

"Ladies and gentlemen: my daughter, Josephine."

Joey jumps out of the cube, lifts her hand and waves to the cheering audience. Then she does something that really takes my breath away. She turns, looks straight at me and smiles. Am I deluded? Did she really pick me out of that crowd in the darkness? All I know for sure is, this girl slays me. I am totally slain. But King Hewitt's just beginning his show.

"I love my daughter," he says, "just like Abraham loved his son Isaac. We're all so terribly flawed."

He looks at Joey with this mournful expression. She gazes back at him sadly.

"Why is love so fleeting?" King says, his voice filled with anguish. "Why can't we trust our hearts?"

I hear heavy breathing. The lady next to me is biting her hand, completely wrapped up in the show. And she's not the only one. The whole audience is on the edge of their seats. King Hewitt waves his cane. The cube mysteriously lowers a little, and Joey steps in. He closes the door.

He waves his cane again, and half a dozen huge, shining swords float down around the box. He grabs one of them and stabs it into the stage. It stands there, gently swaying, embedded in the floor. He takes a short piece of rope out of his pocket and holds it against the blade. The sword slices it like butter.

Suddenly, King yanks the sword out of the floor, and it bursts into flame. He raises the flaming metal over his head.

"Why must we always test love?"

And with that, he pushes the sword through the metal box. His voice is quavering with emotion. He really seems to be shaken up.

"I have no choice," he says, and pushes another flaming sword through the box. Then another and another. The cube is suspended in the air. There's nowhere for Joey to escape to. He's shoving sword after sword through the box at every possible angle, and I swear I can see blood on the blades. I tell myself it's just a magic trick, but I can't help wincing every time King strains to push another sword through.

Finally, he flings open the door. The audience gasps. Because, apart from all the blades sticking through it, the box is empty.

King shakes his head somberly and closes the door. He pulls out the swords one by one. The whole audience is squinting to see if there's blood on them. Maybe, maybe not. One by one, the swords clatter to the floor.

"I promised her dying mother I would always protect our daughter," he chokes out. "As you can see, I failed."

King Hewitt's eyes are shiny with tears. Depressed, beaten, he starts walking into the wings. You could hear a penny drop. Half the people in the theater are scared the show is over. Like what's going on?

Then there's a faint sound. Tapping. King stops. The sound gets louder. King turns, trying to place it. Is it coming from the stage? He listens. The tapping doesn't quit. He slowly moves to the box. Puts his ear against it. Nods his head and opens the door.

She's back. Joey, smiling, waves to the audience. King Hewitt beams.

"Isn't it lucky children are so resilient?"

A thousand people are on their feet cheering. Including me.

When the curtain finally comes down, I'm stunned. Not only was the rest of the show just as amazing (and I'm a guy who hates shows), but the girl of my dreams was up there with the main man. I sit in my seat not knowing what to do next. Most of the people have left, and the ushers are picking up between the seats.

Then it hits me. I'm staggered, but also a little sad. This was like a pre-emptive "Dear John" letter. Joey was breaking up with me before we even went out. She wanted me to see who she was, realize I wasn't in her league and slink away.

As this cold, harsh reality is sinking into my sorry heart, an usher politely interrupts my depression.

"Excuse me, sir, is this yours?"

He picks an 8×10 glossy up off the floor. It's a photo of King Hewitt and Joey holding flaming swords. I flip it over. On the back is written: "Kip, please join me in the dressing room."

Filled with glee, I hold the note up to show the usher, who nods his head. He takes me through some hallways, through some doors, then down a bunch of red carpeted stairs. He's moving so fast I can barely keep up with him. Then he goes through another set of doors, and I find myself alone in a room that's empty except for a big overstuffed couch.

The glee is wearing thin. My head has been twisted around enough for one night. I have no idea where I am or how the hell to get out of this place. Which is foremost on my mind at the moment, because I do not like having my chain pulled. I'm turning to go back through the doors when I hear a voice.

"Did you like the show?"

I whirl. Joey's lying on the couch that was empty half a second ago. I am truly relieved and not a little glad to see her. I smile.

"Very impressive."

"I hoped you'd like it. I was worried you wouldn't come."

"I was worried you were a no-show."

She laughs and sits up, and I join her. She smells good, like fresh flowers. And she looks even better than I remember, which means she's something close to perfection.

"I don't get you," I say. "Why all the games?"

"They're not games. I'm just careful."

"Of what?"

"I want you to know who I am."

"I'm not afraid." I smile.

She looks at me, really deep like she can see into my brain. For a second I think she's as hot for me as I am for her, and I actually wonder if we're gonna kiss right then and there. But a booming voice breaks the moment.

"Aren't you going to introduce us?"

She lets out this little breath, bites her bottom lip, takes my hand and says, "Come meet my father."

Next thing I know, we're in the dressing room of King Hewitt himself. He's sitting in front of a mirror that's surrounded by lights, taking his makeup off. I'm definitely nervous, because I've never met a legend before. I'm expecting him to shake my hand, give me an autograph and send me on my way.

"This is Kip, Daddy," she says.

"Yes! Kip!" He spins in his seat, jumps up and leaps over to me, grabbing my hand. "Come, boy, sit, sit!" he shouts, throwing me into the chair next to him. Then he turns to Joey. "Go on, darling, I'll entertain your young man while you get out of that costume."

She hesitates. "That's okay, Dad. C'mon, Kip . . . "

"Go!" he says to her. "Do you think I'm going to burn the hair off his pretty head?"

Joey smiles limply and tells me she'll be right back. King

Hewitt throws a drink of something into my hand, then raises an eyebrow.

"So what did you think of the show?"

"It was phenomenal. Truly."

King pats me on the knee, then holds up a finger, waving it in front of my face.

"You see, son, it's all about controlling where they look. The human eye can only move so fast, and it only sees so much. A magician plays the margins."

He reaches into my shirt pocket and pulls out a handkerchief. He pulls and pulls and pulls, until he has about ten feet of hanky in his hands. He gets this peculiar look on his face. He takes the hanky and loops it around my neck, then starts to tighten it. I try to stay polite.

"May I ask what you're doing, sir?"

He smiles. "Asking you a question."

"Fire away," I squeak.

"Are you playing the margins with my daughter?"

I blanch. This guy cuts right to the heart of the matter. "No way, sir, absolutely not."

"So what are you playing?"

I'm nervous, groping for words. "No game . . . She's smart . . . she's beautiful . . . "

"She keeps you off balance?" he asks, slightly loosening his grip.

I relax a little. "Yeah, it's kind of unnerving, actually."

King leans in on me, glaring. "You hurt my daughter and I'll slice you up in pieces very slowly without the benefit of magic."

I nod my head, understanding his terms exactly. "No re-assembly. I'll be good, I promise."

King laughs wildly, pulling the hanky off my neck. He throws it up in the air and it vanishes. Then he sits back down in his seat again, completely warm, like we're old pals. I guess I passed some kind of test.

"You're very smooth, I enjoy that," he says. "You're always holding the trump card, aren't you?"

"Is there another way?"

He eyes me, and I feel as if he's seeing right through me. "I think you and I are going to have some fun together, Kipper."

But before I can ask what he means, Joey's back in the room, grabbing my hand and saying goodnight to him. He smiles and waves, and we're out the door.

Joey takes me to the Purple Flamingo Grill, which is known mainly for its decor. The whole place is painted in fluorescent paints and lit in black light so everything glows, including your teeth and eyes. This effect just adds to Joey's looks, since her teeth and eyes are already something special.

I pull out my lighter to light the candle on our table. Joey takes it from me and looks. "It's an old one," she says. "And it's gold. Must be worth a lot."

I nod. "I inherited it," I tell her and leave it at that. It used to be my dad's, the same one he let me play with at the theater a million years ago. It's pretty much the only thing he owned that was worth anything. My mom gave it to me on my sixteenth birthday, said she thought I should have it. I'm not quite sure why, but I have to admit I like it. I get kind of a weird feeling lighting the thing, though, knowing his fingers were once around it too.

Joey orders us some chai, this milky Indian drink. It's usually pretty tame, but this stuff is totally spicy. It lights my mouth right up. "They know how to make it here," she says. "Not as good as we had in New Delhi, but good."

Turns out she's toured all over the world with her dad. In fact, they're going to Atlantic City tomorrow for a three-week stint at a casino there. I get this impressed look on my face and she scowls at me.

"The place is a dive," she says, "filled with drunks and losers. There aren't many legit theaters for magic acts to play in any more."

"What about tonight?" I ask. She explains that the Playhouse owner's an old pal of her dad's, owed him a favor. "It was good to play in town for a change," she says. "I'm sick of traveling."

Joey tells me she's spent her whole life on the road, from the time she was in diapers. Lately, she sometimes spends time at her Aunt Lou's house while her dad goes on jaunts alone. Even so, she has never been in the same school for more than a year, which partly explains why she's such a loner.

"We have something in common," I tell her. "My family's moved around a lot too."

She lifts one of her dark eyebrows. "What kind of job does your dad have?"

"He's not around," I say. "Our moves have been mostly economic, or due to the whims of asshole landlords."

She gives a little snort. "Tough life, huh?"

"Not really," I tell her. "Fact is, we have what we need. That's all I want."

She laughs. "Whoa, a real stiff upper lip." And she reaches over and pinches my lip. "Just checking," she smiles. Then she leans over and kisses me. Take my word for it, it was very nice, especially because I wasn't expecting it.

When I walk her home later, I get another one of those amazing kisses for the effort. The whole way back to my place, I'm like a foot above the cement. I can't stop thinking about how great everything has suddenly become. I meet the most beautiful, incredible girl, and she likes me. A lot. The only down side is I have to wait three long, long weeks to see her again.

CHAPTER SEVEN

The school thing helps take my mind off the wait to see Joey. I have to fill out scholarship applications and knock off a bunch of essays, which I do. But this weird thing keeps happening to my eyes and fingers. We're working on World War Two and I'm writing about the invasion at Normandy, but instead of listing the number of invading troops, I fill a whole page up with Joey's phone number. Or I put down the names of the Allied leaders, and strange combinations happen: Winston Churchill, Joseph Stalin, Josephine Hewitt, Franklin D. Roosevelt. So I delete and start again, but now it's all jumbled up: Winston Hewitt, Josephine Stalin, Franklin Joey Roosevelt. Believe me, I don't usually do this. I pride myself on having a very organized mind. This girl is turning my brain into moosh.

I obsess so much about Joey it even throws me off my game. I actually lose five bucks to Bongo on a hand of five stud, simply because I am thinking about Joey's eyes, not the cards. But that loss snaps me out of it fast. I get back my five and another fifteen from him before lunch is over.

I'm so desperate to get my mind off Joey that when my

mom asks me to go grocery shopping with her, I agree. The minute we walk into the supermarket, I feel like I'm five. There's something humiliating about pushing a shopping cart around with your mother. Especially when she's figuring out the cost per sheet on a roll of TP and asking me if I prefer two-ply or three-ply paper.

"I don't know, Mom, what's the difference?"

"Which do you find softer when you wipe?"

She asks me these questions with a completely straight face and sincerely wants to know the answer. I sincerely reply that I'll go along with whatever works for her, then duck out to check out the fruit juices, where I bump smack into Uncle Ralph. Who knew we'd be having a family reunion in the Big Food Mart?

"Ralphy!" Mom shouts when she sees him. She gives him a big hug. Ralph chuckles. He loves getting those hugs from my mom. He looks at the toilet paper in our cart.

"Ooph, ooph! Gemma, don't waste your money on three-ply!" he says.

Mom looks stricken. "Don't you think it's softer?"

"No," Ralph the World TP Expert replies. "It's all in the density. Buy the two-ply."

"Lucky you were here!" Mom smiles and exchanges the twelve-pack in the cart for the one Uncle Ralph has pulled off the shelf. Believe me, I hope I never live long enough to become a toilet paper gourmet like these guys.

Uncle Ralph looks at me. "So, we're seeing you tonight at six sharp, Kippy?"

"As always," I reply.

Mom goes all serious. "How's he doing at work, Ralphy?"

"How's he doin'? How's he doin'? Your kid is my best waiter, my wine steward, my number-one employee. How do you think he's doing?"

My wacky uncle gives me a hip check that sends me crashing into the paper towels. Mom grins. "He's carrying a 92 percent average in all his classes this term too."

After some deliberating, Uncle Ralph puts four twelve-packs of two-ply TP into his shopping cart. "Do I look surprised? Should I look surprised? The kid has more brains than all of us put together. When he gets his MBA, he's gonna franchise my restaurants. Put a Golden Goose in every city in North America. Make millionaires out of all of us. Right, Kippy?"

This is a new one to me, but I've learned over the years that all most adults require is a humble smile and a nod. So I smile humbly and nod. Uncle Ralph is thrilled by my response.

"Do I love your kid? Do I love my nephew?" Before I can stop him, he grabs me and kisses me on the cheek.

Ralph gives my mom another hug, then takes off with his shopping cart. Just as he's rounding the corner into the meat section, he turns and points at me. "Remember, Kippy, six o'clock sharp. Be on time or I break your legs!"

Mom shakes her head. "I love that man," she says happily.

These are the kinds of distractions I'm reduced to in my lame attempts to stay sane. Because, when I'm on my own, I can't control myself. I know Joey's not home, but my finger keeps punching out her phone number on the dial pad. Then

I listen to her voice announce that nobody's in right now, please leave a message. I do this pathetic ritual about eight thousand times. I go prowling around her house, looking at it from the back lane, trying to figure out which window is her bedroom. I don't break in so I can smell her sheets or anything. I'm no psycho. But I admit that the thought passes through my mind. If that means I'm crazy, so be it. The truth is I am crazy—about her.

Finally, the big day comes. When the three o'clock bell rings, I deke past Bongo and a group of goofs he's assembling, bolt out the crusty old doors of the school and head straight to her house. I bet myself twenty bucks she'll be there.

Her house is no mansion. But it's a posh-looking two-story item in a decent neighborhood. By decent, I mean her neighbors' lawns are manicured and they all use their blue boxes, which are neatly filled with recyclables on garbage day. On my block, people recycle their blue boxes too: as street hockey goalposts, storage bins, laundry baskets, kitty litter boxes. The uses are endless.

When I arrive, I don't skulk around. Certain Joey's there waiting for me, I head right to the front door. I ring the bell. No answer. I ring again. Still no answer. This time I knock. And the door swings open.

"Hello?" I yell, but everything's quiet. I step inside and call out her name. There's just silence, so I stick my head into the living room. What a place. Theater posters everywhere. King Hewitt performing in Paris, Copenhagen, Berlin. Photos of him with all kinds of different old famous guys. And a whole wall filled with pegs that hold magicians' top hats. There's gotta be at least thirty of them. I go in for a closer look. Some of these hats are pretty ancient. I try to resist, but my hands start reaching for one. I pick it up and peek inside. No rabbits. I decide to try it on. It fits. I glance in the mirror. I guess it'd look better if I had on a tuxedo with tails. That's when I hear a voice.

"Brilliant choice!"

I turn to see King Hewitt grinning at me. I quickly pull off the hat and am all apologies, but he won't hear it.

"That hat, young Kip, was worn by the great man himself: Harry Houdini. Remarkable. Your head is the same size as his."

I feel my skull, trying to figure out if it's big or small. I have to admit I'm a bit rattled by the guy. When I work up the nerve to ask if Joey's around, he tells me she's in the bath. So, while we're waiting, King gives me the grand top-hat tour. He's been collecting them his whole career, top hats that once belonged to the greatest magicians of all time. I can't stop myself from asking how much the collection's worth.

"It's priceless," he whispers, "utterly priceless." Then he raises a bushy eyebrow, just the way Joey raises hers, and says, "It was rather bold of you to walk right into the house."

"The door was open," I say. "It seemed like I should check things out."

King laughs. "You're the kind of fellow who likes to take chances, aren't you?"

"It's the spice of life," I say without a thought, and smile.

King pounds me on the back, chuckling. "We're cut of the

same cloth, you and I, Kipper. I could tell the instant I set eyes on you."

I'm flattered, but I'm not quite sure what kind of cloth he's talking about. Then he makes an invitation. "Kipper, tomorrow I'm taking you for lunch. Can you be ready at noon? Don't tell Jo."

"Uh, sure," I say. "What's the big secret?"

"It's not a secret. It's a surprise."

I nod. "Okay then. My lips are sealed."

This is a guy you have to love. A star, somebody the doors open for, and he takes me under his wing. What does the King have in mind? To drill me some more about his daughter? To invite me into the show? While I'm pondering the possibilities, Joey comes down the stairs. She looks incredible. She stops halfway, her face completely blank, and says, "So there you are."

"So here I am," I say. I'm wondering if she hates my guts or something. "Is that all right?"

"I can live with it," she says, cracking a little smile. I feel like the sun just broke through the clouds and is drenching me in bright, warm light.

Joey and I go to the lake for a stroll on the beach, and she tells me all about Atlantic City. Not about the casinos and the shows she and King did, but about her walks on the boardwalk and how the sea smells alive and dead at the same time and how high the waves were during a storm. This lake we're looking at may be big, but compared to the Atlantic Ocean, it's a drop in a bucket. She tells me she has this fantasy about crossing the ocean in a thirty-foot sailboat, living off the fish she catches and battling ten-foot breakers and gale-force winds. That sounds pretty cool to me, and pretty soon we're fantasizing about buying a boat and sailing all the way to New Zealand and Papua New Guinea. Okay, it's true I've never been in a sailboat before, I'm not quite sure where Papua New Guinea is, and I get spooked just thinking about the ocean. The thought of bobbing around in a little boat with whales popping up or a giant squid wrapping its tentacles around the hull scares the total hell out of me. But I don't mind dreaming. As we walk, I imagine being with Joey in the middle of the Pacific, lying on our backs on the deck after surviving a terrible squall, staring up at the sky, just us and a trillion million stars winking down.

I figure I'm about the luckiest guy on the planet. I've got a girlfriend who takes me all over the universe in more ways than one, and her rich and famous father is treating me, Kip Breaker, to a swank lunch tomorrow. I am more than lucky. I am a walking horseshoe.

CHAPTER EIGHT

I've got a study block right after lunch, so the timing is perfect for my date with King. I wait in front of the school for him, but he's late, and I'm just about ready to go back inside when a shiny yellow BMW pulls up. King waves me in, and I plop down on the leather seat. It smells new.

I figure we're headed for some downtown bistro, but instead he guns it onto the highway. There are only truck stops for the next thirty miles, and I start to get a whiff of nerves. Is King some kind of psycho? In a second, though, I realize he's anything but.

"How do you feel about the equine species, Kipper?"

"You mean, like horses?"

He laughs. Big. "Not mere horses, my boy. I'm talking about steeds, stallions, mares—the descendants of Pegasus."

King may talk like some kind of bizarre Englishman, but suddenly I begin to understand him when he points at the overpass. "I love that bridge," he says. "Such a gentle structure."

The bridge is nothing special. What's great is the sign attached to it: PINEWOOD TRACKWAY EXIT. I start grinning ear to ear. He was right. He had me totally pegged.

"Is this lunch? The races?"

"But of course, young Kip. There's no better aid to the digestion than the company of horseflesh."

We pull up to the track, and an attendant opens King's door and greets him. King tosses the guy the keys and a fiver and starts galloping toward the stables. I'm running to keep up.

"Hurry, Kip, we're going to the backside!"

I follow him, and pretty soon we're tiptoeing around piles of hay and big puddles of water. When we get to the barn King's looking for, he charges inside, with me close behind. Instantly, I'm hit in the face with the sickly sweet scent of fresh manure, and it's all I can do not to gag. I manage a polite smile as King introduces me to the trainers, the jockeys, the grooms, the exercise riders. He knows everybody, and they all suck up to him, treat him like the king he is. The whole time he's flashing this huge wad of bills, giving tips to stable boys for bits of information as they go over the *Racing Form* with him.

I don't feel like getting too close to those horses. They're big and nervous, and who knows when one will break out and go crazy on the first human it sees? They're beautiful, but I read somewhere that inbreeding makes them temperamental. It must be weird to be bred just for running. Break a leg, get a bullet in the head. Tough life.

King, with a gleam in his eye and a hush in his voice, calls me over.

"Look at her, Kip. She's been blessed by the gods."

He's pointing to this horse called Dancer, who actually

seems pretty ratty to me. She has a white stripe down her snout and red-brown hair—that is, what hair is left. A groom is applying cream to some bald, sore-looking patches.

"Don't mind the skin condition, Kip. Look into the eyes of a winner."

I gaze into Dancer's big browns and try to see something. I come up short. If there's a winner in there, it eludes me.

"She looks great," I say. My lack of conviction triggers a huge laugh from King.

"You're like all the others," King says. "That's why she's rated at 50–1."

With a big, knowing wink at the trainer, King drags me out of there. We pick up some jalapeño dogs and head to the betting windows. King puts some money on the counter and says, "Dancer to win."

He takes my elbow and gazes into my eyes. "This is a rare tip, Kip. Do it."

I take the two bucks my mom gave me yesterday and spend it on the lunch special, even if she is a bit mangy. King may talk like he's from another planet and act like he never got off the stage, but if he says this horse is sure-fire, I have to at least give it a shot. He pulls me up into the stands, waving to this guy, slapping hands with that guy. It's a great feeling, sitting there in the sun, looking at the field.

Then I hear the announcer. "They're away!"

It all happens so fast. These big horses shoot out of the gate with these little jockeys hanging on. Dancer's in third place, and King has a wistful expression.

"She's a beautiful horse," he sighs. But I'm sinking inside as the announcer is blaring over the speakers: "It's Ruby Slippers in the lead, Jack Hammer on her heels and Silver Dancer pulling up the rail."

He's got one of those nasal voices that sound completely phony. Nobody cares, though. They're all locked in the race.

One little old lady is leaning so far forward in her seat she actually falls and bottoms out on the cement floor. Like nothing happened, she instantly bounces back up and starts yelling: "Hammer! Hammer! Kill 'em! Hammer!"

I'm not much better. By now I'm howling too, and King has joined in: "Do it, Dancer!"

"Come on, baby, come on!"

And then this amazing thing occurs. This lousy, half-bald nag starts pouring it on and takes over second. The announcer sounds like he's having heart failure. Come to think of it, we are too.

I'm moaning, "Please, please, please!"

And King is growling, "Go! Now! Do it!"

Then it happens. At the home turn, Dancer hits her stride. Kicks in down the straight and thunders past Ruby Slippers. She wins by two lengths! King and I are screeching, hugging. He's holding me up in the air and shaking me.

"I told you! Tips like that are gold, diamonds, the rarest of the rare!"

He plops me back in my seat, and then it hits me. A kind of cold, awful chill moves through my body.

"Fifty to one! I can't believe I only bet my lunch money."

King puts his arm around me.

"Never second-guess yourself, Kipper."

I gaze at him, trying to understand. "I know you got a good tip," I say. "But how did you really know she was a winner?"

King stares out over the track, the stands, the crowd, like some liege surveying his kingdom.

"I studied her, checked her record and the jockey's record, talked to the trainer, considered the other horses." Then he gets this faraway look in his eyes. "And Lady Luck was smiling."

I smile too, despite the sad realization that I could have made much, much more. "What a great idea for lunch."

King nods and bites into his dog. "I could never understand people sitting there, simply eating, when they could be making productive use of their time."

We see eye to eye on that one. That's why I always have card games going in the cafeteria. Something's nagging at me, though. I know I shouldn't open my mouth, but the question just pops out.

"If you don't mind me asking, how much did you win on that one?"

He holds open his ticket and I take a peek. I almost fall head first onto the concrete floor. He bet two hundred. At 50–1, that's ten thousand dollars.

"It's just a game, Kipper, just a game," King says. Then, before my very eyes, he slowly and methodically rips his ticket up into little pieces.

I can't believe what I'm seeing. "Are you crazy?" I yell. "Don't do it!"

King shakes his head. "You can't learn to win till you're prepared to lose it all."

"But ten grand!"

King considers my protest, even though it's a little late.

"Perhaps you're right . . . "

He reaches into his palm, where he's holding the torn-up pieces, and pulls out the ticket. It's completely whole again.

"This time, we'll take the win," he says, and gives me that big, dazzling smile of his.

I thought I was a big man, but I am amateur hour. Kid's stuff. This guy really *is* the King. A total genius. I could have stayed there all day watching him, learning, making money, but I have to catch the bus back to school. As I leave him there at the track, he waves me off with his blessing.

"And Kip, I'm using my winnings to buy a surprise for Joey. So you didn't see me."

"You're the invisible man."

"How about lunch here again next week?"

"Sure thing," I smile.

"And one of these days, my boy, you and I are going to hit the casino."

"You can get me in?"

King just laughs his famous laugh, and I feel a little stupid asking the question, after what I've seen today. A little stupid, but a hundred bucks richer.

CHAPTER NINE

Talk about horseshoes up your butt. Things for me couldn't be better. I have King showing me what being a high roller is all about—and I have Joey.

Spending every spare minute I've got with her has taught me a few things. Her favorite haunt is the park beside the lake. She likes walking for hours on the trails or on the beach in hard rain with her head uncovered. Says she can feel the raindrops on her brain. When we study together (she's going to score a scholarship for sure), she drinks double espressos with no sugar and eats fresh cut-up grapefruit with salt on it. She hates her real name, Josephine. Says it sounds like an old brand of soap or something.

But she's definitely not old soap. I get dizzy looking at her, though I can't let her catch me doing it. She hates being stared at. And if I tell her she's beautiful, she gives me this look that could flatten mountains. She hates flattery. So I just think it.

"Have you seen this one?" We're at the park on a Saturday afternoon. Joey waves a handkerchief. She's always practicing new tricks. In a blink, the hanky turns into a cane. By now, I'm becoming nonchalant.

"Nice cane. Can you turn it into a crutch?"

She starts chasing me around the pond with the cane, beating on me, until we fall into some daisies by the edge of the water. I go to kiss her, but she's busy retracting the cane and sneaking it into the false pocket in her jacket.

"Why do you practice all the time?" I ask her.

"Habit, I guess," she shrugs. "It's the only thing I could ever do with my dad. Learn the business."

That's the most she's opened up with me since we met, so I decide to press on. "When did your mom take off?"

"When I was four."

Now this is weird. For me, that is. Because when I was four, my dad went zoom too. I tell her we share some history, and she replies, "I always thought four-year-olds were cute. Why would our parents freak and run?"

My own dad, Kipling Senior, didn't freak and run. More like gasped and fell. But since I'm not much into talking about him, I ask if she's ever heard from her mom.

"Total vanishing act. You?"

"Something like that."

I'm not sure why I don't want to blab to her about my dad, since I'm so curious about her family. But not much about my dad bears repeating. What do I tell her? That my dad was a semi-unemployed house roofer? That my best memory of him is the smoke rings he'd blow around my head? How about him dying broke, without insurance, leaving my mom screwed forever? See, I don't think these things bear repeating in company. I think the best thing I can say about my dad is nothing.

I remember him lifting me up in the air, muttering something to me, then his face twisting up. He tossed me to Uncle Ralph, grabbed his chest and crumpled to the ground. Lucky my Uncle Ralph was a good catch. I might've been just four, but I can still see Dad's twisted-up face and him lying there, all gray. For years I thought he died because I was too heavy. My mom kept telling me it wasn't my weight that killed him, it was cigarettes. If that's true, it's kind of ironic that the only thing I have of his is the gold lighter he used to light his coffin nails.

I guess Joey can read it in my eyes. "What are you thinking?" she asks.

But instead of pouring my heart out to her, I just say, "Teach me a trick."

She shakes her head no. "Secret information."

"Oh, come on, you told me how you did that popcorn trick."

"I just gave you a clue."

I start biting her fingers, her arm. "Oh please, please, please . . . "

She hesitates, and I start clicking my teeth together like Jaws. She weakens.

"Don't tell my dad."

"Never," I say, and I feel this sick little twinge. Now I'll be keeping secrets for both of them.

She pulls a new handkerchief out of her pocket and throws it in the air.

"Meet my pet hanky."

The hanky floats over to me. Then she says, "Go, Spot! Attack!"

In a flash, the hanky is fluttering in my ears, my eyes. I push it away, but it's like a giant crazed butterfly. I try to run from it, but I can't get away. It covers my face. I pull it off and it's on me again, plugging up my nose, my mouth.

"Stop it!" I yell. "I give up!"

"Here, Spot. Heel."

The hanky floats gently over to her and drops into her hand. She pats it. I'm gasping for air. After I recover, I say, "So teach me how you did that."

"Sure. I'll do it again. Watch closely. Ready, Spot?"

"No, Spot, heel!" I shout. Then, feeling kind of limp, I mutter, "I'll pass for now."

She laughs. I have to admit she trumped my biting-the-arm gambit. We sit back down in the flowers, and I give the hanky a tentative poke with my index finger.

"Did the King teach you this?" I ask her.

"When I was five," she replies.

I'm in awe. By the time I was five, the only thing anybody had taught me was how to brush my teeth. "It must be so great having him for a dad."

She gives me that look of hers that could freeze pools of lava.

"What's the problem?" I ask her. She shrugs. I know I should leave well enough alone, but when I know I've pushed somebody's button, and I don't know what the button is, I get curious. It's like picking a scab. I can't stop till it starts to bleed.

"Is it 'cause he's away a lot?" I ask.

She nods her head yes. Emphatically. "For sure."

I'm starting to catch on.

"You don't mean traveling, do you?"

Joey breathes. This is clearly not something she likes talking about. "He gambles."

I play surprised. Very surprised.

"You're kidding," I say, layering in a slight tone of curiosity for credibility's sake.

"Big time," she says, apparently not detecting an iota of insincerity in my response.

"The guy's an illusionist. He must win all the time."

Joey lets out a bitter laugh. "Nobody wins."

"Of course they do."

"Just enough to keep them playing. Whatever the game, the house controls the odds. They want you to stay playing, 'cause eventually you have to lose it all."

I can't help but be a bit incredulous. If what she's saying is true, her dad's a stooge. And King Hewitt is definitely not a stooge. I guess she can see what I'm thinking, because she starts telling me a story.

"One night my dad came home after midnight, stinking of booze and smoke, with a big smile on his face. I was ready to skin him alive because he emptied out the coffee tin before he left. All the grocery money was gone. Again."

I'm hearing what she's saying, but I'm having trouble getting my head around this grocery money thing. Her eyes flash "stop thinking and listen." So I do.

"He really turned on the charm. Threw a handful of cash into the coffee tin and told me I had him all wrong, he was coming from a brilliant night, a superb night. That didn't mean anything to me, because I knew what could happen the next day. But no matter how hard I was on him, he didn't flinch. He just stroked my cheek and called me Princess, and then he handed me a large gift-wrapped box. A present for standing by him, he said."

"What was it?"

Joey gives me this look like I'm totally thick. "Don't you get it? I'd heard that a million times before. He was just trying to buy me off. Except he was being different this time. He swore that the present was to mark his last bet. He'd finished gambling for good."

"And you believed him?" I ask, feeling totally boggled.

"I studied his face, trying to decide if he was for real. He told me he understood my suspicions, because he'd taken me on so many roller-coaster rides up till now. But then he started to cry, said he was sick of the ups and downs, felt horrible for what he'd put me through. He'd had a great night, the night to end all nights. And he showed me the receipts for the bills he'd paid off, the bank statement with the deposits he'd made."

"He was gonna quit while he was ahead. Makes sense to me," I say, playing along like a champ.

Joey shakes her head. "I felt this terrible weight lift from my chest. He was truly going to turn his life around. He asked me to 'honor the moment' and open the present. Inside was a leather Roots jacket."

"Those things are worth a bundle," I say, thinking she'd look great in one.

"I tried it on. It was a perfect fit. I loved it. It was more than a jacket, he said. It was a Promise. Then he put his hands on my shoulders, moved his face right up to mine and swore that from that moment on, he'd never wager another penny."

Though I already know the answer, I feel obligated to ask the question. "Did he really quit?"

"Master illusionists make you believe what you want to believe," she says. "A few weeks later I couldn't find the jacket. Searched every inch of the house. It was killing me, because Dad had been so wonderful since the night he gave it to me. He'd been home most of the time, apart from going to the odd solo performance. He was putting all his money in the bank. He even cooked a bouillabaisse."

"You were afraid losing the jacket would put a curse on it all, weren't you?" I say, feeling torn in two by what she's telling me.

"Yeah. I couldn't sleep, I couldn't eat, I was totally stressed. Finally Dad noticed it. And gently, really sweetly, he asked what was bothering me. So I confessed that I had lost the jacket. I couldn't find it anywhere."

"Was he mad?"

"No. He nodded, listened. Then he shrugged it off, told me not to worry. But I couldn't let it go. I explained to him that I loved the jacket, it had a very special meaning for me. He just patted me on the shoulder, told me that it's a terrible mistake to become attached to fleeting material possessions. 'The Lord giveth, the Lord taketh away,' he said."

"What a great guy," I start to say, but the words get caught in my throat when I see her giving me that look again.

"You just don't get it, do you? He wasn't being great. He uses that line all the time when he loses," she says. "So that's when the penny dropped. I looked him in the eye and asked him point-blank what he did with the jacket. He didn't try to hide it, just casually mentioned that he'd had a little cash-flow glitch. Said that soon he'd be doing a week at the Royale and then he'd pick the jacket back up."

I'm a little confused. "Pick it back up? What does that mean?"

Joey's starting to get upset, more upset than I've ever seen her.

"He pawned it. He pawned the Promise. And that's when the truth really hit me: he hadn't stopped playing for one second."

I breathe really carefully, not wanting her to detect anything in my reactions.

"He showed me the pawn ticket, swearing that as soon as he was flush, he'd buy the jacket back. Then he capped it all by explaining that he had done it for my own good. The jacket was too dangerous."

"Dangerous?" I ask.

"Yes," Joey tells me, fighting the emotion. "He said he read it in the papers, kids stab each other for jackets like that."

"He told you he sold it for your own protection?"

She looks away from me, her voice sounding choked. "I felt like killing him or killing myself. I was so hurt. I thought I was going to break in half."

"What did you say to him?"

Joey's face gets tight. "I thanked him for being so thoughtful."

I let out a hard laugh. "That must have stung. What did he do?"

"He kissed me on the forehead and said 'you're welcome,' as if he'd just done me some great favor."

I'm totally staggered by this story. I feel so bad for her. And I'm shocked to discover that King Hewitt isn't as successful as I figured. But it gets worse. She tells me that almost everything they own has been mortgaged or pawned. When King works now, it's just to pay off debts.

I let her know that her situation sucks, that I didn't realize what she was going through. I'm practically crying myself. I'd do anything to help her. I don't want her to suffer like this.

She takes a short breath and says that the whole betting thing makes her nuts. I swallow hard when she says she doesn't want it in her life. I can really understand that, after what she's been through, and I say so. She throws a rock in the water and says gambling is the government's cash cow. They cut taxes and then put in more casinos. I know what she means. It's a total scam.

Then she explains why she's totally into the grades at school. Because she knows if she doesn't get a full scholarship, she'll never get out, never get free. Even if she does get a scholarship, she'll have to make sure her dad doesn't get his hands on the money. He'd go through it in an hour.

"I understand," I say. "You've got to protect yourself."

All of a sudden she stands up and lets out this manic banshee cry. I look at her like she's only a little crazy. She shakes her head.

"I can't believe you actually got me telling you all this crap," she says. She looks pretty disgusted with herself.

"That's okay," I reply. "I'm glad you told me. I'm completely sorry you had to go through all that."

She gazes at me with those I-could-sink-into-them-forever eyes and asks me if I truly understand.

I nod. "I think I do."

"Because I've never told anybody. I never trusted anyone enough."

Before I can reply, she reaches into the grass and picks up this big brick that's sitting there, all grown over with weeds. Just a tiny bit worried she's gonna throw it at my head, I ask what she's doing.

"One of the first tricks my dad ever taught me. The brick. Heavy as rock. Feel the weight."

I do. It's a brick, all right.

"Concrete and bricks, the foundation of a good house. Solid. Strong. Reliable. People build their lives on these things."

Then she taps the brick and it breaks in half. "He was a good teacher, don't you think?"

I can see how upset she is, and I rub her neck, tell her that I'm there for her. "Joey, when you're with me, you can forget about all that crap."

And we kiss. For a long time. I'm like floating in the clouds, sailing over mountains, surfing down the streets of Bliss City. Being with her is amazing. Better than anything I've ever felt or imagined. Greatness.

But I'm thrashing on the horns of a romantic dilemma. We go to different schools, so she doesn't know what I'm really into. If I tell her the truth, she'll blow me off for sure. Understand, I'm not just playing her. At least half of me isn't. I feel like I'm Dr. Jekyll and Mr. Hyde. Split in two. Part One of me is right there for her, hating what her dad does and what he's done to her. Part Two of me is totally pumped about continuing to meet her dad so I can learn some new moves. One thing I'm totally certain of, though: I am 200 percent, completely, fully, incredibly, in love with this girl.

CHAPTER TEN

In between school, work and spending time with Joey, I've been managing to hit the track with King at every opportunity. There haven't been any major scores like the first time, but I just follow his lead, bet where he says, and the wins keep happening. I'm feeling a little bad about doing this behind Joey's back. I'm feeling even worse about the stories she told about her father. They're nagging at me, so one day I ask him if he ever lost big time.

He smiles. "Everybody hits rough spots, Kipper, that I can't deny. But you of all people know you can't win if you can't lose." And then he puts down five hundred bucks on Red River to win and walks away with three thousand bucks. I'm telling you, the man defines awesome.

Before too long, King brings up the casino again, and of course I can't resist. On the day we've arranged, I take off from school at lunch and head over there. Once I'm on the bus, I pull a sport jacket and tie out of my pack and put them on. I figure the outfit ages me up at least a couple of years, so maybe I won't get ID'd. While I wait for King I'm thinking about what Joey said—and I have to say it doesn't make sense to me. I mean, I've seen the King in action. I saw him score ten Gs. Him broke? A loser? Impossible. Okay, maybe he's had some down times. But I'd bet 100–1 that they didn't last long.

"Kipper!"

I turn to see King Hewitt charging up to me, raring to go. He shakes my hand, then pulls on my ear (don't ask me where that came from) and says, "Did you bring your stake from the track?"

"Plus a bundle," I reply. "I almost shot myself for not putting more down on that last horse."

King slaps me on the back. "You're the real thing, Kipper. You have killer instincts."

"If you're afraid to lose, you can't win."

King smiles approvingly. "Truer words never spoken. Welcome to my castle."

He swings open the door of the casino and, with a grand sweep of his arm, waves me in. Just like at the track, everybody in the place is delighted to see him. He tips the doorman, flirts with the coatcheck lady, disappears the security guard's badge and reappears it on the manager's butt. They're all laughing and hooting. They love this guy, he's the best. King is right. This is his castle.

Everything's shining silver, reflecting mirrors and dazzling lights. There are hundreds of slot machines, big rooms of high-stake card games. The whole main floor's filled with bingo tables, and a giant glowing screen is flashing the numbers. Roulette tables are everywhere, dice are flying, and long-legged ladies sparkling in sequins are handing out drinks and food and making change. There's this hypnotic rumble I'm hearing through it all: the sound of money. It's like being inside the most incredible, brilliant kaleidoscope. I'm just sort of standing there, gaping at the beauty of the place, wondering what took me so long to get here, when King pulls me around the corner and shushes me.

After all the razzmatazz of us walking in, I'm taken by surprise when I see how quiet he suddenly is. I watch his eyes. He's utterly focused, like a martial artist, standing and studying the action.

He's honed in on two slot machines. One has a guy in front of it; he's pushing coins in and blowing cigarette smoke. The other machine has this stooped little old lady feeding it metal. Her back's all humped over, and her fingers are bent and twisted. She can barely raise her arm to put the money in, so she does it real slow, leaning on her walker the whole time to get the right leverage. After watching these two intently for maybe ten minutes, King speaks.

"Which of those slots would you say is hotter? The gentleman's or the elderly lady's?"

I take another long look at them both while I ponder the question. Then I lay down my theory. "The man's got an ashtray full of butts. I'd say he's been pumping that machine full and it's ready to give."

King snorts. "You're not paying attention."

I look again at the guy. He's got one new cigarette burning in the ashtray and another in his mouth. I nod. Now I get it.

"He's chain-smoking. Two at a time."

"Whereas," says King, "the elderly bird drinks quite slowly."

I check out the old lady. She's got about a dozen empty tomato juice glasses sitting on top of the machine.

And now I see that she's fumbling with her purse. She doesn't look very happy.

"Count to ten and she'll be gone, Kip. I'd say she's just about finished this month's pension check."

I count to ten, and right on the mark, the lady grabs her walker and hobbles off. In a blink, King and I have grabbed the machine and he's stuffing coins into it. He pulls the arm and nothing happens. He keeps doing it, again and again. And while he's doing it, he tells me the first thing to know is that the odds are impossible. I've done a bit of research on the machines and reply that I read it was like a 92 percent return. He explains, very patiently, that it's an 8 percent guaranteed loss on every bet. The casino skims eight cents off every dollar wagered. Over time, you're certain to lose it all.

"Then why are you playing if it's impossible to win?" I ask him.

"That's what makes it interesting. My whole life has been about doing the impossible. I hunger for it, don't you?"

"You know it."

His fingers are unbelievable. It is amazing how fast he can feed money into that machine. Hundreds of bucks being swallowed up with no return. The change ladies can barely keep up with him. After about an hour of watching him lose, I ask him if he's all right. He grins.

"I'm not losing, I'm getting ready for the winning. Feel it. Put your hand there."

He's pointing at the belly of the machine. I hesitate a second because this seems a little weird.

"Do it."

I lift my paw and spread it, palm down, on the machine. I'm not quite getting the point of the lesson, but I'm trying. Then he asks me if I feel it. Being the honest type, I admit that I'm not sure.

"Concentrate!"

Not wishing to aggravate him further, I close my eyes and try to feel inside the machine. This is *definitely* getting weird. But I do start to feel a faint sensation.

"There's something like a buzzing."

"Good, good. Keep focusing. Underneath it, do you sense a soft hum?"

Maybe I'm crazy, but I try to make like my hand is an antenna or something. And then it happens. There's this gentle vibration going through my palm, up my arm.

"I feel it!"

King happily pounds me on the back.

"That's the sign! She's so full of coins, she's ready to burst."

He reaches into his pocket. Pulls out a coin.

"This is the one. This coin is the detonator."

"How do you know?"

"Feel it. It's humming too."

I hold out my hand. He carefully places the quarter on my palm. I close my eyes, trying to feel the weight of the coin in my hand. There's nothing at first. But then, really faintly, I start to sense the vibration. This is the coin, all right.

King plucks it out of my hand and holds it up to the light, like it's some sacred object. He waves it in the air, then puts it in the slot. For a second, nothing happens. Then the machine starts going crazy. Lights flashing, colors whirling. One orange, two orange, three oranges line up. Three in a row. The bell starts to ring and — five coins fall out.

I can't believe this is happening. I hit the machine, figuring it's some kind of mistake. But no, that's it. Five. Frustrated, I turn to King, but he's chuckling.

"Oh, she's a fickle one, isn't she? A mind of her own. Okay, darling, I'm giving it all back to you."

He takes the five coins and pushes them through the slot. Pulls. Nothing happens. Nothing. If it was my money, I'd be kicking the thing, screaming at it. But not King Hewitt. He just laughs.

"What a tease!" Then he turns to me and holds out his hand. "Kipper, loan us a fifty. I'll double it back to you."

I immediately reach for my wallet. What the King wants, the King gets.

"No problem, King. I wouldn't have it if it weren't for you."

King takes the fifty from me and buys some rolls of coins from a passing hostess. He squeezes the rolls between his hands, then opens them, and coins fill his palms. He starts stuffing them in the machine and pulls. More coins and more pulls, again and again. I look at my watch. He goes through fifty bucks' worth of coins in less than four minutes. They are all gone. And he's laughing like it's a great joke.

"This machine's an enchantress. A goddess!"

Then he does a one-eighty and stops laughing, gets this determined look on his face. He holds out his hand.

"Give us another fifty, Kipper."

I mean, that look is scary. The guy could drill holes in mountains with that look. Without hesitating, I find a hostess, hand her the bill and bring King the rolls of coins she gives me in exchange. He slaps the rolls against the machine. As coins fall out from beneath his hand, he flicks them with his free fingers into the slot. Once they're all in, he turns to me.

"This is it, Kipper, the moment of reckoning."

He pulls the arm. The machine whirls and whines. I can hear that faint vibration ringing in my ears. It rings. And one stupid little coin drops out.

But King is smiling. He takes the coin. He puts it up to his eye. He smells it. He licks it. He polishes it with his handkerchief. Now I'm starting to catch on.

"Is this the one, King?"

"No doubt. This coin is the key to unlock the gates of heaven."

He pinches the last coin, the Coin, between his finger and thumb and delicately inserts it into the slot. I hold my breath as he slowly pulls the arm. The lights flash, the pictures whirl.

And stop. Nothing.

I'm staring. I can't understand it. I completely believed, I felt the vibration, I saw the Coin. I'm devastated at his loss. But

King? He's laughing. To him, losing is just the flip side of winning, part of the same package.

"The Goddess of Gambling's an ancient goddess, Kip. She demands sacrifice that must be offered freely and with grace. Complain, and she will strike you down."

No complaints from me, even if he did lose my money. After all, I scored a hundred on the first horse he gave me, plus a couple hundred more on the other ponies he tipped me on. He's teaching me more about the slots than I'd ever learn on my own. Besides, when he's flush again, he'll pay me back. Double. It's a total win-win situation.

CHAPTER ELEVEN

When I was a little kid, not long after my dad died, I started getting this aching in my legs that kept me up at night. My mom said my whole body was changing, called it "growing pains," and she'd massage my legs till I fell asleep. In a way, I feel like it's happening again. Only this time I don't need my mom for anything. No pain this time, either, because it's not a physical change. It's mental. I'm functioning at a new level. My brain's completely partitioned, so I can multitask like crazy. The amount of stuff I do in a typical day is staggering. Between school, work, Joey and the odd visit to the casino, I'm feeling a little like Superman.

I've even been to the casino a few times on my own. I was a little nervous at first, but it turned out that since the staff had seen me in there with King, there was no problem. They look at me like a regular now. Nobody blinks.

I only turn up there once a week or so, though, on a weekend afternoon if Joey's not available, or an off night from work. I try my luck at the machines and don't do too bad, either. Usually I break even. I can play for hours and make my money last. I've started working out my own system based on King's "feel it" method.

I love the casino. It's like a rock concert without all the noise. Maybe it's a spiritual thing. The vibration that takes you away. It makes you wonder. Here all these years I thought I was an atheist or something. I guess I'm a religious person after all.

Bongo corners me one day at lunchtime.

"Kip, Kip, you're gonna die, man, you're gonna die!"

He's got a grin on his face so huge it would crack the skin on a normal person. Luckily for the Bong, he has plenty of extra flesh on his cheeks, so he's safe from harm. I ask him what's the cause for celebration.

"Little Mike had his birthday yesterday!"

"Wow," I say, "how incredible. You must love him very much."

Bongo nods his big head. "Sure I love him. He got his presents in cash. And he's sitting at the poker table as we speak."

"How much do you think he has?" I ask, barely interested.

"At least fifty bucks," Bongo replies. He's literally salivating at the prospect. "Maybe more. Like seventy. Let's go!"

I shake my head and tell him I have to pick up some books in the library.

He is appalled. "What's wrong with you, man? A month ago you would've killed for the chance to clean Mike out. Now everything's that girl or your books."

"What can I tell you?" I say. "I'm going through some changes."

Bongo eyes me, not quite buying my explanation. "I know you, man. Something else is going on."

I shrug. "An education is a precious thing," I say, then add another cliché: "And true love doesn't come along every day."

Bongo looks at me with newfound respect. "You're profound, man. You're the deepest guy I know."

I give him a pat on the shoulder, instruct him to leave Little Mike at least five bucks of his birthday money, and send the Bong on his way. What I don't tell him is the real reason I'm not going to play, which is: The stakes are too low. And there's no buzz in fleecing Little Mike; it's too easy. Besides, why would I want to sit under the fluorescent tubes in that scuzzy cafeteria when I can have the casino's sparkling lights instead?

I go to the library and start hunting down some books on the invasion of Normandy, but it's no good. I can't get the casino out of my mind. I don't want to be here, I want to be there. I try to imagine explosions on the beach and artillery blowing landing ships out of the water, but it doesn't work. The detonations turn into the slots ringing and pouring out money. I look at the clock. Barely past noon. I grimace.

The librarian comes over and gently asks how I'm doing. "You look as if you're in pain or something," she says.

I'm about to tell her I'm fine when my mouth takes over. "Yeah," my mouth says, "my stomach's been bothering me."

Worried that one of the school's top students may be suffering from an ulcer, she sends me immediately to the school nurse. My mouth tells the nurse that I have cramps and a headache. She's very sympathetic and nurturing and sends me home to rest.

Miraculously, the second I get to the bus stop, all my

symptoms disappear. It seems that it wasn't a physical issue after all. I am having a spiritual crisis that can only be cured by going to my place of worship, the house of pretty lights.

It's true that in less than two hours I lose a hundred and fifty bucks. But I'm not complaining. I can't tell you how great, how free it feels to be in there. Best feeling in the world.

It isn't like I was planning on increasing my visits to the casino. But as it turns out, Joey gets assigned a gigantic project for school, so she doesn't have as much time to hang out with me. This gives me a hole in my schedule that I have no choice but to fill. I begin making more pilgrimages to the sacred shrine. At the same time, my stomach condition starts to worsen, perhaps from "the intense pressure of maintaining my grade point average." My teachers are very understanding, and I find it a simple matter to leave school early so I can get a good chunk of time with the slots.

There is one catch, though. Once you're working a machine, you're loath to abandon it before it pays out. So I'm finding more and more that I have to call Uncle Ralph and beg off work, also because of the intense pressure of maintaining my grade point average.

After a good month of this, I have to say I'm pretty buzzed. All I'm thinking about these days is those pretty lights. Joey and I haven't had much luck getting together, but we talk on the phone late at night, when we're both in bed. We lie in the dark and pretend we're sailing the ocean in our thirty-foot sloop, headed for Polynesia. Joey doesn't know it yet, but our yacht is no dream. I'm an inch away from scoring it. A couple of big nights and we'll be sailing away.

My second month into my new sacred experience, I turn the lock on the front door, walk in, and my mom's sitting there in the living room, waiting for me. She's got the look on her face she used to get when I was a kid and I came home late and she figured I'd been hit by a car or kidnapped or fallen into a hole someplace.

"Kip, I was so worried. Uncle Ralph said you didn't show up for work. You'd better phone him."

I look at the clock, and I can barely hide the shock of it. I've transcended time or something. It's totally bizarre. The clock says it's past eleven, but I feel like I was in the casino for five minutes. In fact, the last two months feel like they happened in the last half hour.

"Oh no!" I say. "I can't believe I forgot to call him. I was at the library cramming for my physics exam."

She isn't very happy to hear that. She's always been down on cramming. Her advice is to study a little every day, so that when the big exams come around, you just have to review. She knows an amazing amount about effective studying techniques and has spent seventeen years drilling it into my head.

"I wish we had more time together, Kip, but now I'm in such an awful rush, I'm late for my other job . . . "

"Don't worry, Mom, I already ate."

"And I have to get to the bank machine tonight. I have to put in my paycheck, your college fund deposit . . . "

Why does she do it to herself? I know why. Because of me. I give her a little hug.

"I go by the machine on my way to school, Mom. Why don't you let me make the deposits from now on?"

Her face instantly brightens. I just took a big weight off her shoulders. It's weird. She kills herself for me and I barely thank her; I do the tiniest thing for her and she lights up like she just won the lottery.

"Could you? Oh thanks, Kip. Here's the card. The PIN's eleven seventy-seven."

I smile. Lucky number. I wish she'd really get a lucky number sometime. She sure deserves it.

I watch Mom put her bag in the car and drive away to her night shift. I'm feeling a little blue about her. My mom's a saint, and I worry about that. Because you know what happens to saints.

I go to the bathroom to take a leak, and I see myself in the mirror. I look pretty good. A little demonic, but good. My eyes seem huge. I figure that's due to all the neon in the casino and the fact that I've been surviving on mainly Pepsi and hot dogs for the last two months. Nothing that an excellent meal at the Golden Goose couldn't fix. My face is a bit pale from lack of exposure to daylight, but that'd be cured by a couple of hours in a suntan studio. Or better, a day at a tropical beach. That would be good, I think. I make a big score and fly Joey and me to Hawaii. Rubbing each other with oil, sipping cool drinks, sliding and snorkeling in the water. Then the phone rings.

A half-hour before midnight, and it's ringing off the hook. It's gotta be Joey, calling for the goodnight chat. I run into my room, dive over the bed and grab it. But it's not her. It's her dad.

"Kipper! Kipper, luck will have us both!"

"You have something cooking?"

"Yes, my friend, a little soufflé in the oven. A pony."

"As in a hot tip?"

"It transcends hot. This is a tip that burns holes in hands."

That sounds very good indeed. King may not have a golden touch with the slots, but when it comes to horses, he is invulnerable. Every time we've been to the track, I've watched him study the form. I've seen how he gets a close-up look at the actual horses, pals around with the trainers and jockeys—and has his ear to the ground.

"How big a hole, sir?"

"Thirty to one."

I do some quick arithmetic.

"Ten dollars makes three hundred."

"One hundred makes three thousand," calculates King. "Five hundred makes fifteen."

"And so on," I say, feeling weak. He's making these numbers gnaw at my guts and I'm hurting, I'm feeling the hunger. A very feeble sound emerges from deep in my belly.

"You're giving me this?" I ask him, somehow hoping that he'll say he's just pulling my chain. But he's not.

"Bring two five-hundreds to the track at ten tomorrow. One five for you, one five for me, which I will quickly double back to you."

I start going over these numbers in my mind. I start getting very queasy.

"All I have is a hundred," I say. "Could we do fifty and fifty?"

I hear King chuckle.

"Sorry, Kipper, it's five and five or nothing."

I stab a pencil into the table. I feel like a medieval torture victim being torn in two on the rack.

"So you want me to come with a thousand at ten a.m.?" I ask. I know how stupid the question sounds, but the whole thing is making me crazed.

"You'll leave," he says with absolute certainty, "at ten-thirty, with sixteen thousand dollars. Tax free."

I take the phone receiver and pound it into my chest. This is the opportunity of a lifetime. I'm being offered a gift of biblical proportions. But then reality, like a bucket of vinegar-laced water, pours over me.

"I'd have to dip into my college fund," I say.

"Only momentarily," King replies lightly, without losing a beat.

"It'd be wrong," I say, feeling a little like a Sunday school teacher. But at the same time, I know I can't do it. I don't want him to lose respect for me, to think I'm a wanker or a tourist. He cottoned on to me in the first place because he could see what I had going. I have to squeeze out of this without losing face. But my panic is unfounded. King, being the gentleman that he is, realizes what he's doing to me.

"You're right, Kipper, how crass of me. Those kinds of savings are sacrosanct. Untouchable. What kind of demon am I to tempt you? Forgive me, son."

I hear this with great relief. I could never look my mom in the face again if I dipped into that account. On the other hand, I don't want to be cut out of any future action that King might have going. I mean, if he hadn't needed such a high stake to cut me in, I'd have done it in a flash.

I sigh. "So you understand."

"Utterly. I apologize for the intrusion. In atonement, I'll put down ten for you. At ten."

He hangs up. I take some ice out of the fridge, lie on my back on the floor and put an ice cube on each eye. I sometimes do this when my mind and my body are in deep conflict. Every time King's told me to bet on a horse, I've made money. And the first time I was kicking myself for not putting down more. The odds this time might not be as great, but 30–1 is nothing to whine about.

Water's dripping down the side of my head and the ice cubes slip off. I wipe my face with a dishtowel and look at the time. It's a quarter to twelve. I bet myself twenty bucks that I can dash over to the bank machine for Mom, make her deposit and be in bed by a quarter after.

I like the streets pushing midnight. Especially on weekdays, when everybody's tucked down. They're all dreaming and snoring, and all that sleep energy seeps out of the houses and soaks the atmosphere. The trees and grass and bushes are all frozen in it, and I feel like I'm the only moving object for miles. So peaceful.

Okay, it's a fantasy. It's a bunch of crud that puked out of my head. But when I'm walking that way, it does feel like I'm the last human on earth. The last human on the planet with a bankcard. His mother's bankcard.

I hold the card in my hand and look at the bank machine. The little red sign says OPEN. I punch in the pin number, 1-1-7-7. I push DEPOSIT, then OTHER ACCOUNT. I take the envelope, put in my mom's paycheck, and make my mom's deposit into the college fund.

The machine makes this sweet-sounding chime. And, good computer that it is, asks me a completely innocent question: DO YOU WANT ANOTHER TRANSACTION?

My heart starts beating fast.

It seems so simple. King's offer requires me to come up with a thousand. But really it's only five hundred, because the other five is a loan that he pays me back immediately—doubled. And my five hundred is multiplied by thirty, so that makes . . . sixteen thousand dollars.

If I scored that kind of cash, what would I say to my mom? Nothing. I'd open another bank account, so she'd never know. And I wouldn't tell Joey. I couldn't ever.

Sixteen thousand dollars. I roll the number around in my mind fifty or sixty times. And every time I come up with the same answer. No.

My mom slaved to earn this cash. And I slaved to earn a piece of it too. That fund is too special, too important. I promised her I'd never touch it. And I won't. Because it's wrong. Because she trusts me.

Besides, the bank machine only allows you to take out five hundred a day, max. And look what time it is: 11:59 p.m.

My blood stops running in my veins. The timing is too perfect. My finger moves toward the button. I grab it with my other hand and squeeze. Grip my finger hard, like I can force the terrible urge out of it. Harder, harder. The treatment starts to work. The hunger is starting to fade.

BEEP BEEP BEEP.

My head jerks up at the sound, almost breaking my neck.

It's the bank machine, reminding me to do something. The screen reads: END TRANSACTION?

Before I can stop it, my freed finger flies, hitting everything in sight. It punches the NO button, the WITHDRAWAL button and then . . . the $500 button.

Ten crisp, clean fifty-dollar bills emerge from the slot. I stare at the money, stunned. What just happened? How did my finger manage to do all that so quickly? I mean, I hardly blinked. It was a mistake. It only happened because of the bank machine's hideous beep.

The only thing to do is redeposit the money. I pull out an envelope, put the cash in. I know it's a little risky to deposit cash, but this is too important. I have to put it back in. Cover my finger's mistake. I know it's my finger, not me, because King wants a thousand, not five hundred, and five hundred's the daily maximum and—

I look at my watch. The second hand clicks past the twelve. It's midnight. Today is now tomorrow. A new day. A new daily maximum.

My right finger starts twitching, moving toward the machine. I shove it in my pocket. Holding the envelope in my left hand, I lick the flap and close it, then hold the envelope in my teeth while my left index finger, the one I can trust, the one I can control, moves to push the DEPOSIT button.

But my left finger keeps moving toward the WITHDRAWAL button. Even when I step back, the finger keeps reaching. I try to grab my sleeve with my teeth, but then the envelope drops out of my mouth. I step on the envelope so it doesn't get blown away or dog eaten, but while I'm looking down, the right hand leaps out of my pocket, rockets straight for the bank machine and punches the buttons.

Another five hundred dollars peeks out of the slot. Defeated, I take the cash, put it in another envelope and turn to go.

BEEP BEEP BEEP! I freeze at the sound.

I whirl, wondering what the machine wants to do to me now. It's the card and receipt. I yank them out of the machine and my eyes lock on the withdrawal statement. My black deed staring me in the face. I pull out my dad's lighter and set the receipt on fire. I hold the flaming paper till it singes my fingers. Maybe that'll teach them.

I scoot home, the thousand bucks in my pocket throbbing like a living heart. I hate being out at this time of night. I'm paranoid about getting jumped. Everywhere I look there's people walking behind me, in front of me. Beat-up cars with weird dudes peering at me. I hear footsteps coming real close, getting closer. I pick up the pace and turn the corner, figuring

I'm dead for sure. But it's just some lady, at least forty or something, carrying a shopping bag from the 24-Hour Store. She smiles at me. A lot like the way my mom smiles at me. It sends a chill down my spine.

I get into the house, and the good news is it's fourteen minutes past midnight—I won the bet with myself. My mom won't be home till dawn. I rip off my clothes and jump in bed, slipping the cash under my pillow. I can't sleep. I keep thinking about what I did. Is this really so bad? The chance to more than double my bank balance?

Before my dad kicked off, he was a roofer, taking whatever work he could get, even if it meant laying down shingles in the middle of winter. I bet if he'd had a sure shot at sixteen grand he'd have grabbed it in a flash. Mom once told me he never gambled, but why would he tell her the truth? In the end, I guess he died with the secret. Maybe his ending was a bet, too, a last big one with the sky. Like King says, winning's only the flip side of losing. My dad just lost the flip.

CHAPTER TWELVE

I wake to the sound of the front door opening. It's dawn, and my mom's finally back from work. She's creeping around super quiet, trying not to wake me up. I might be awake, but I'm not much in the mood to talk to her. What would I say? Hey, Mom, check out the currency I lifted from our bank account! I hear the floorboards creak as she bends over carefully and takes her shoes off. Then she tiptoes up the stairs and goes into the bathroom. I hear the water run as she washes her face. Hear her gargle when she brushes her teeth. The bathroom door opens, and she pads softly like a cat across the hall.

I snap my eyes shut just as she sticks her head in the door for a loving look at her wonderful son. I don't know why I'm beating up on myself. The money'll be back in the bank before noon. My biggest problem's gonna be making up some excuse when she sees the bank statement.

I wait another half hour, till I'm sure she's asleep. Then I get up and go. It's barely seven o'clock, but I can't stay here. I've got ants in my pants.

I tuck the thousand bucks in my socks and go outside, pondering a deep question: should I go to school today? I could cut my first class a little early, claiming stomach pain, then bullet to the track. After the race, I'd make the deposit, set up a new account with the winnings, and be back in time for the rest of my afternoon classes.

Not much point in showing up for one morning class, though. Besides, it's Mr. Cheese, which is risky. I could fall asleep and miss my appointment with King. So: no school this morning. What about the afternoon? I'll come back for sure. I've never cut more than a class or two. Yeah, but do I really want to sit still the whole afternoon listening to teachers twiddle their brains when I've got sixteen Gs burning a hole in my pocket? Forget it. Instead, I'll set up the new account, put, say, fifteen thousand in it. With the cash in hand, I'll shop. Pick up something nice for Mom, maybe a necklace or a fancy pair of shoes. Get Joey some boat shoes, a yacht sweater and a life jacket.

I'll tell Mom it's a pre-emptive birthday present. And Joey? Our four-month anniversary.

Thinking about our four-month anniversary makes me decide a little romantic breakfast before Joey goes to school would be just the ticket. By seven-thirty, I'm at her place. I figure King's still asleep, so I don't want to ring the doorbell. But she's got to be up by now.

I peek in the kitchen window, and I see her walking across the hall with a fluorescent orange toothbrush in her mouth. There's even a little foam trickling down her chin. I tap on the window. She looks up. Her eyes bug out, and she runs into the bathroom. A second later she emerges, face wiped, toothbrush gone. She gives me a dirty look as she opens the front door.

"Isn't this a little early for you, stranger?"

"Sorry about catching you with the toothbrush."

"What toothbrush?" she asks. Then she looks at my shirt pocket. "Oh, that toothbrush."

I reach in my pocket. There's a fluorescent orange toothbrush, wet, sticking out. I brush her nose with it and invite her out for a pre-school munch.

"I don't have time for a whole breakfast," she says, grabbing the toothbrush back from me.

"Then how about coffee and a doughnut?"

We go to Horton's Cafe and sit in the back booth with our crullers and coffee. Joey's got this funny look on her face, which makes me a little nervous, because I definitely do not want her reading my mind. Or materializing an object in my socks, which are crammed with fifty-dollar bills. But I am obligated to inquire about this expression, because she's staring at me with her nose pinched up.

"So what's the look all about?" I ask, casually stirring my usual three spoons of sugar into my coffee.

"I'm trying to figure you out," she says. I'm now experiencing Grade-A nervousness. This morning's action is something I definitely can't share with her, unless I want her to do a permanent vanishing act on me. Poker is not my game, but the main thing I've learned from playing it is how to hide what I'm holding. So I keep up the bluff.

"You don't know what day it is?" I ask, a slight tone of hurt in my voice. Take note, this is an important tactic. If you want to keep your interrogator off balance, put her on the defensive. Joey is not easily rattled, but the question certainly gets her off the topic of me, and I can see her puzzling, probing, trying to remember what day it is. I just keep chewing on my cruller nonchalantly.

Finally, she throws her hands up in the air. She's stumped. This is good.

"Happy four-month anniversary," I say, handing her a bunch of daisies. They're a little crumpled from being stashed in my jacket, but they could be rare orchids, the way she gapes at them. She melts, which is not something she does very often. This warm, happy smile beams from her and she reaches across the table and takes my hand.

"I hate anniversaries," she says and kisses me. I'm floating over the table, over the cafe, in the clouds, it's just me and her, there's nothing else except the two of us and the rest of the world can go stuff itself. It's pure, perfect bliss.

"D'yous want some more java?"

I look sideways and see Horton holding the coffee pot. He's not exactly what I meant by bliss. Horton's the grease-covered, half-bald cook in this place. There's a big, tarnished gold bull-ring hanging between his nostrils.

We shake him off and I move to kiss her again, but clearly Horton destroyed the moment. She gazes at me, drawing a line on my arm with her finger.

"Let's get out of here," she says.

"Okay, I'll walk you to school." But she hesitates. She's considering not going to school today. Today, she's considering spending our anniversary with me.

"What will we do?" I peep, trying to keep my voice from cracking.

"We'll think of something," she says, squeezing my arm.

Remember what I said before about my great tactic of getting her off balance? Forget it. Now I'm caught between a rock and a hard place. If I turn her down with some lame excuse like school, she'll be hurt and think I'm a loser. But if I tell her the truth, that I'm meeting her dad in an hour, she'll never speak to me again.

"Oh, God, I'm sorry," I say lamely. "I have a big exam first thing."

I see a trace of disappointment on her face. But mine's as bad, believe me. Spending the whole day close to her—I couldn't think of anything better. Well, maybe one thing.

"What's the test?" she asks.

"English," I lie. "Mr. Cheese is grilling us on *Othello*."

"Love. Betrayal. Death," she nods. "That's one way to start the day."

"Yeah, isn't it?" I play glum, praying she won't ask me any questions about the play, given that I've never read the thing.

I walk Joey to her school. We hold hands, but the buzz is gone. I killed it. Love, betrayal, death. I guess Shakespeare had it right.

As soon as I see her disappear through the doors, I rocket straight to the express bus and just make the connection. I'm at the track by a quarter to ten, heart pounding, lungs aching, panting for breath. I look and look, but King's not anywhere.

"You didn't let me down."

I nearly jump out of my skin. It's King. Where he came from, I have no clue. By now, I don't worry about these things.

"I have it," I tell him and pull out the money.

"Nerves of steel. I knew you had it in you," he says, plucking the grand out of my paws and leading me in. King tells me that our horse, Sisyphus, is deaf in one ear, so everyone counts her down and out. Not only that, she lost the last fifteen races she was in. But the trainer tipped King that the horse had worms, and since they've cleaned her out, she's been burning up the track, running record times.

"No one can touch her," King says. He gives the money to the cashier, all on Sisyphus to win. He hands me my ticket for the five hundred, and we go to our seats. I'm looking at the track, the crowd, the anxious faces, and feeling a bit smug.

Next to me is this guy in a suit with gray hair who's biting his nails down to the bone. He's got his *Racing Form* all marked up, but it's obvious he doesn't have a clue. I can tell from the way he's dug his pencil into the paper that he's frustrated, he's behind, he's chasing the money. Probably everything he owns is riding on the next race. *Our* race. But he's stacked it all on the wrong horse, because he doesn't have the inside track. He doesn't have King guiding him along, King digging the dirt, King glad-handing the lackeys, King getting the goods.

I'm still thinking about what to buy for my mom. She deserves a cut for having fronted me the money, even if she didn't know about it. Plus, I'd like to do something to cheer her up. She works too hard. Her jobs are burning her out. But if I get too extravagant, she'll wonder where I got the money. So I'll say I got an amazing tip at work, which is almost the truth, and take her for a nice dinner. She'd like that. A glass of Pouilly-Fuissé, some glazed salmon with black butter sauce. My mom deserves to be treated like a queen after all she's been through.

"They're off!"

I nearly fall out of my seat at the sound. King grips my knee.

"These are the moments worth living for, Kipper!"

I'm yelling, "Sisyphus! Sisyphus! Sisyphus!" and it's incredible, this pony is moving up fast. Even the announcer is going wild, his voice crackling over the speakers.

"It's Guinevere in front, Pinochet a neck behind and Sisyphus coming up fast. Yes, that's Sisyphus . . . that's Sisyphus in the lead!"

King is clenching my knee so hard I have to take his wrist and shake it off. He puts his arm around my shoulder.

"Did I tell you? What did I say?"

"You're it! You told me!" I yell as the horses make their final turn, heading into the stretch. Sisyphus is a good ten feet ahead of the pack. I'm drooling, I'm dreaming, I can't believe it's for real. The announcer is fevered, his voice screeching into the stands.

"It's Sisyphus in front, Sisyphus! Pinochet in second, Guinevere third . . . "

We're on our feet, screaming for Sisyphus, our horse, our baby. She's bringing the money home. I'm jumping, pointing, shrieking for this miracle pony.

"Sisyphus! Sisyphus! Sisyphus!"

She's sailing, flying, a hurricane, unstoppable. What a tip! What a horse! What a day!

And then the world cracks in half.

About twenty feet from the finish line, Sisyphus kind of wobbles, slows down. Can this be real? Am I hallucinating? I smack myself across the cheek, squeeze my eyes hard together and open them. But it's real.

Pinochet crosses the line first.

King and I hit our seats in the same instant. We sit staring out, not comprehending what's just happened.

"And it's Pinochet, Sisyphus, Guinevere," yells the announcer, but it's as if someone's turned the volume way down. I feel like I'm a million miles away, watching all this through high-powered binoculars. I see the color flush out of my face, see my hands clutch my knees. I hear a sound come out of me—a low, terrible moan. I can't find a way to move my mouth around words that could describe how damaged I'm feeling. This is the worst.

It's different for King. A little giggle comes out of his mouth. Then a chuckle. Then a huge, blasting laugh. He pulls on my ear.

"It's a beautiful thing, isn't it? Pure art."

I stare at his grinning face. I am bewildered.

"What art?"

"The slender thread that fate dangles us by. The irony. The drama," he replies.

"I just lost a thousand bucks," I say.

"Not to worry. I'll pay you back my half in no time."

"When?"

"Soon, Kipper, soon."

I blink and he's gone. And slowly, slowly, I reel myself in, put myself back in my body and stare at the track. I don't move for a long time.

CHAPTER THIRTEEN

I'm up all night making lists, calculating the solution. By the time the sun comes up, and my mom gets home from her night shift, I've worked out a good approach.

My plan of attack is this:

1. Hang onto the bankcard. If Mom asks for it, remind her that it's much easier for me to make the deposits.
2. Win back $500.
3. Get paid back by King.
4. Redeposit it all in the account.

It's a simple, four-part plan. Elegant in how it can be achieved. Nothing to it, really.

Notes on execution:

A) Monitor the answering machine to beat Mom to it, in case of calls from school, etc.
B) Intercept all bank statements.
C) Minimize contact with Mom to avoid all questions.
D) Maximize time in the casino.

The casino is a critical part of the plan because it provides everything I need:

a) Food (nourishment, etc.)
b) A bathroom (toilet and sink for washing)
c) Opportunities
  i) To win $$$
  ii) To find King and get $$$ back

Estimated length of time required to achieve objective: 24–48 hours.

I know I can win back my five hundred in a couple of hours, actually in a couple of minutes. But I'll need to stick around the casino to the max to have any hope of spotting King.

The next morning I forge a note from my mom explaining politely to the principal that, on top of my chronic stomach disorder, I've got food poisoning from a tainted burger, and I'll be back in school the minute I stop projectile vomiting. I drop the note in the office mailbox before school officially opens. The janitor's the only one there, and I don't think he knows who I am, but just in case, I wave pathetically at him and limp out of the school holding my stomach. Then I head over to Horton's and wait for the casino to open.

I'm sitting there, drinking a glass of milk and eating some toast because my stomach feels weird, when I detect a hand on my shoulder. I stiffen. Can this be the cops? Am I somehow being busted for using the bankcard? Then I sniff the air. Faint hint of bologna, scrambled eggs and catsup. Only one person in the world has that odor at eight a.m.

"Hi, Bongo."

Bongo plops down across from me and looks at my toast.

"No thanks, Kip, I already ate."

Bongo, Prince of Bologna, has heard through the vine that I'm hanging with some high-stakes dude, have been cleaning up. How did he hear this? I wonder. He reveals that somebody spotted me with an old guy outside the casino. Is this all true? he asks. After all, it kind of adds up, with me never joining the poker game any more, or any other wagers, for that matter. Not to mention the sport jacket and tie I'm wearing. I give a little grudging shrug.

"You gotta take risks to win big," I say.

"That's what I keep telling myself," replies Bongo somberly. Then he arches his bushy eyebrows and leans in on me. He's still got a little catsup in the corners of his mouth. And there's a half-chewed piece of bologna on his sleeve. This is the slob who's pushing in on me for information.

"How'd you meet this guy, Kip? Why's he helping you?"

"Bumped into him, a fluke," I say. "He's a nice man."

"What's his name?"

"Herman Klachefsky," I reply. Bongo nods, taking a mental note of the great man's handle.

I'm relieved that the Bong doesn't know who my mentor is, and I'm determined to send him looking in the wrong direction. I have to. If Bongo finds out it's King Hewitt, it'll be all over the airwaves. Everybody will hear. It'll spread across the city like mayonnaise. Joey'd have to be in Timbuktu not to get the information in her face.

But Bongo won't let up.

"Let me go out with you guys. So I can learn something."

I eyeball him, gravely probing his face.

"Mr. Klachefsky's a very old, very secretive man, Bongo. And he's not terribly well."

Bongo's ears perk up, and I notice a little dried catsup on one of his lobes.

"How much time does Mr. Klachefsky have left?" Bongo asks, no doubt wondering if there's still time for him to squeeze in a session.

I shake my head sadly.

"His circulation is failing. His right leg was amputated last spring. Gangrene. His left leg's next. I have to push him in his wheelchair. The doctors say he's got less than a month."

Bongo is distraught. His potential guru has a foot in the grave.

"You shouldn't take the burden on yourself, Kip. Let me push the chair."

As Bongo says "push," a chunk of scrambled egg flies out of his mouth and lands on my arm, which doesn't help soften my stance in regard to his request. I flick the egg across the table and shake my head.

"It's just not possible," I say.

"Please please pretty please!" begs Bongo. And every time he says the P, another piece of scrambled egg goes flying.

"Stop!" I yell, and hold my finger up. Bongo freezes. Then I get this strange inspiration. Maybe it was the hailstorm of egg bits that triggered me, but the words come fully formed out of my mouth without a thought.

"Bongo, if you're serious . . . "

Bongo nods yes, very solemn, very serious.

". . . you'll need a stake to be involved."

"How big?" Bongo asks, ready to rock.

"You'll have to give the cash to me for safekeeping. You take the bets as Herman calls them. That's the only way to learn. You're guaranteed to quadruple your initial stake. Minimum. Could go higher. Much higher."

His eyes light up. This is the deal he's been waiting for. This is the deal he's been dreaming about.

"Okay, okay, okay, I'm in. How much?"

I pinch my lips together, letting him hang on my pause. Then I say it.

"One thousand bucks."

All the blood in Bongo's upper body drains into his feet. A confused, disappointed, childlike expression appears on his chalky face.

"I don't have it," he squeaks.

I'm filled with regret.

"Sorry, pal, but he's a stickler for the stake. Mr. Klachefsky's whole philosophy centers on the Risk. You can't win a lot unless you risk a lot."

"I understand, I do," says my badly shaken Bong. "I guess I'm just not in your league."

I pat him on the shoulder consolingly. My gambit seems to be working. I want him to back off, to get out of my face. If I tell him to get lost, he'll just push harder. So I give him what he wants, to be offered an In. The price is high, and I'm sure he'll walk away, tail between legs—which is what he does.

As he plods off, feeling like he just wimped out on the brass ring, I consider what my response will be if he actually comes up with the money. That'd be very fine. I'll take it, replace it in the account so I'm square with my mom—and worry about the rest later. Either way is cool with me. I win the bluff or I bluff the win.

Once Bongo's out of sight, I check the time. The casino opens in fifteen. I nab a bus over there, and I'm practically the first guy in line. Behind me, at least a hundred people are lined up, chomping at the bit to get in. All kinds of people. Old bag ladies, rich guys in suits, working stiffs, walking stiffs, you name it. Everybody's dying to get in there. But nobody's dying more than me.

The doors are unlocked and I charge in, followed by the herd. I let the stampede whoosh by while I question the staff about the King's whereabouts. Nobody's seen him for at least the last couple of days. I zoom over to the slots and touch each one, trying to feel the Vibration. Most of them feel very dead, limp, not keyed at all.

Then I get a funny sensation. I see a purple machine sitting by itself, the lights flickering like something's not quite right. I feel it with my hands. I concentrate. Beautiful. It's an oil well, a gold mine, a swollen river.

I'm gonna make every penny back on this baby. Every cent, and it'll take a half hour, no more. The only thing that will slow me down is putting the money in and pulling the arm. I reach into my pocket and a cold wind blows over me. I'm broke. I was cleaned out at the track, that's why I'm here.

And I spent my last couple of bucks on toast, milk and bus fare.

I have no choice. I have to hit the college fund so I can play. I can see the bank machine from where I am standing. There's already a bit of a line-up, and it's getting bigger. My problem is, how do I get the cash without leaving this slot machine? The minute I slip away, somebody is sure to grab it and score the payday that should be coming to me.

This is the moment when I wish I was Elastic Man and could stretch the distance between the two machines. It's really biting my ass: why don't these idiots just use their heads and set up the slots to accept bankcards? That way you'd never have to worry about reloading. You'd be plugged right in. Now that would be progress.

I breathe, calm down and have a cool look around me. Then I see it. A machine just down the aisle has an OUT OF ORDER sign on it. I quickly grab it and stick it on mine. Go to the bank machine and take out a hundred bucks. Hustle back to the slot and start the feed.

DING DING DING.

In a flash, I win. I'm up fifty bucks on the first pull. Once was a time I would've bragged about a haul like that for a week. Today, I'm thinking, good start, ten more like that and I'm home free. And I know I can get it, because the money's in there, just waiting for me to ask. I ask again and again—

And again and again and again and again and again—

I look at the clock. This is good. I've only been here ten minutes, I've got tons of time to break her. And I will. Except that I need a refill.

I put the OUT OF ORDER sign up and hit the bank machine for another hundred. This round I know I'll score. And I do. First pull is worth thirty bucks, the second brings in twenty, then forty—I'm on a roll.

But then she starts taking some back, and all of a sudden I'm deep-sea fishing, pulling on a giant marlin or hammerhead shark, giving her line, reeling her in, trying to tire the big fish out. Everything's good, I'm in control. In a second she'll be beat.

Instead, the line breaks, and she swims away.

I'm shaking my head. This fat stupid machine just swallowed another hundred. I have to laugh. The machine is playing me. We both know she's ready to spill. But it's not going to be easy. This is going to take a lot of patience and smarts. To walk away now would be kissing goodbye to the two hundred I've invested so far. One more round, a couple more pulls, and the big one will come. It has to. It's inevitable. I put the OUT OF ORDER sign up again and head to the bank machine. This back-and-forth thing is driving me nuts, screwing my rhythm. No wonder it's taking so long to win it back. So I stick in the card and take out three hundred to break the curse.

I breathe. Flag a hostess and get a coffee and fries. I inhale them and then face my metal friend for another round. The lights are flashing in a weird kind of pattern. I'm starting to wonder if it's some kind of message. If I could interpret it, I'd know just how to pull, just the way to drop the money in so I can turn this around. I stare at the lights, put my hand on the machine, feeling, sensing.

Then it hits me. This machine works in patterns of five. The lights are flashing five, the vibration works in five-second rotations. I think back. Was I scoring every fifth bet? Not every time, but I'm pretty sure the biggest paybacks were on the fifth try. So I feed it a couple of bucks on the first four pulls, and on the fifth pull, I do twenty.

DING DING DING.

I score a hundred bucks. It worked. *Die, Machine. I broke you. You are mine.*

I shortchange the next four tries, just like before. On the fifth pull I load it up even bigger. My arm's getting tired, feeding the thing. And what do you know? The tricky fish eats it.

I go an hour like this, back and forth, back and forth. And then I'm flat again. I put up the OUT OF ORDER sign and scoot to the bank machine. Put in the card and the screen says: SORRY, YOU HAVE REACHED YOUR $500.00 LIMIT.

Am I happy? No, because I want to keep going. My money is in that iron beluga and I want it back, I want what's mine. I'm standing there, trying to figure a way to get some money out of the bank machine, when the guy behind me asks if I'm finished. And I guess I am. For today.

As I walk away, my heart sinks. Somebody's moved the OUT OF ORDER sign, and that old lady with her walker, the one I saw the first time I came here, is at my machine. She's taken over my spot.

I start to laugh. People look at me as if I'm nuts, but I don't care. Because, like King says, you have to appreciate a great performance when you see one. I got beat by an enchantress. I should be grateful to have met that kind of power. My biggest mistake was wanting it too bad, feeling desperate. I felt guilty about seeping from the college money, and so I behaved like a loser. And lost. It won't happen again.

Moving to the exit, I consider my situation. Now I'm fifteen hundred bucks in the hole. It would be better, much better and wiser, not to dip into the college fund again. And I won't have to if I can track down the King.

I walk out. I barely have enough change in my pocket to catch a bus home. As I'm dragging myself to the bus stop, there, slathered on a telephone pole, like an answer to my prayer, is King Hewitt. His picture, that is. On a poster. Now I know why he's not in the casino. He's performing tonight! I wonder why Joey hasn't mentioned it. Could she be pissed at me for not seeing her so much? I shrug off the creeping doubts, because I am feeling very optimistic. All I have to do is call in sick to Uncle Ralph and head to the Savoy. I'll catch King after the curtain comes down. The only trick will be cornering him in his dressing room without Joey spotting me. He'll be flush because he's going to be paid big-time for the performance. Hewitt, being a man of his word, will probably double me up like he promised. It'll be nothing for him to do it. And I'll be nearly square again.

I'm a bit awestruck, pondering Hewitt's words about the Goddess of Gambling. Complain and you are punished. Keep the winning attitude and you win. All I have to do is stop whining and start laughing and the answer to my problem appears smack in front of my nose.

Life is a beautiful and mysterious thing, isn't it?

CHAPTER FOURTEEN

My first attempt at sneaking into the Savoy Theater is a bust. An usher spots me walking in without a ticket and politely stops me. I can't say my ploy was elegant, but I was trying for the direct approach. Then it occurs to me that there may be an easier way.

I go to the box office and determine that there is an intermission at nine o'clock. With that information, it's a simple thing to wait for the break. I come back a little before the hour, and when people pile out to drag on their cigarettes, I fold into the crowd. After ten minutes the lobby bells start ringing, and I wander in with everybody else. I bet myself ten bucks that they won't be asking for ticket stubs on the return, it's too much of a hassle. I win the bet and tuck into the old theater.

But the place is pretty packed, and I'm getting nervous because I can't find a seat. I go upstairs and check out the balcony. I spot an empty seat and sit down, praying nobody's going to show up waving their ticket in my face. Then it happens. A guy steps up to me glumly, looks at his ticket. I get this sinking feeling, but he's not looking at me. It's the lady next to me. She apologizes, scoots up, and he sits down. I'm on a roll. Not only have I scored a seat, I'm in the balcony, so there's no chance Joey can spot me from the stage.

There's the blast of a trumpet, the house lights go down, and suddenly spotlights are combing the whole theater. People start waving their arms, trying to put their hands in the light. Kids are bouncing in their seats with excitement. The curtain opens, and the whole crowd goes "oooooo" in unison. In the middle of the stage is a gigantic column of fire. Joey strolls out from the wings. She looks incredible in this long black gown. She's holding an unlit torch that she puts inside the fiery column. She pulls it out, blazing flame.

She puts the torch in again, deep inside the burning column. Pulls on it. It won't budge. Tugs again, and a pair of hands are holding on to the other end. I can hear people gasp. She yanks hard, and King Hewitt steps out of the fire. The audience goes nuts, applauding, whistling. King takes a big swooping bow.

"Fire is our brother, our sister, our mother," King says. "I was born of it."

He waves his arm, and the column of fire disappears. I'm sitting there thinking how great he is when I realize his sleeve is smoking. He doesn't appear to notice it, but Joey does. She quickly smothers it with a cloth.

King laughs. "Don't worry, child, smoke is the spirit. The immortal part of ourselves."

Then, all of a sudden, smoke's pouring out from his hair, his sleeves, his shoes. He opens his collar and more smoke chimneys out. He waves his arms, and now smoke's seeping right out of his skin. The crowd's whooping. They love it.

Joey takes a big cloth and throws it over him. She pulls it off . . . and he's gone. She looks for him, but he's not there. Slowly, the cloth, which she threw on the floor, starts to rise. Everybody's eyes open wide as King, grinning, steps out.

For some reason, he stumbles on the cloth. He recovers quickly, but for a flash he seems to lose his smile.

He brushes off the glitch and waves his hand. "Ladies and gentlemen: The Buddha said the source of all sorrows is our attachment to worldly things. What are you attached to in this world? What things in your life can you not let go of?"

A giant silver platter appears over the audience and slowly floats toward the stage. Lowers itself before King. On it is a painted egg. And a bill.

"For me," says King, "a priceless porcelain Fabergé egg given to me by my father. And a 1905 one-thousand-dollar bill, worth much, much more to a collector."

Joey shows the egg's certificate of authenticity to the audience, and volunteers are invited to come on stage to examine the bill and the egg. They're all suitably impressed. Personally, I just want the show to be over so I can collect my money. I spot a little smoke still coming from King's back. But he doesn't notice. He's too busy working the crowd.

"With these extraordinary possessions," King says, "I will begin to chase away my sorrows."

He reaches out, and Joey hands him a hammer. He holds it high and waits till every eye is pinned on the mallet. With a sudden exhalation, he brings it down, smashing the egg. The lady next to me groans. Next he lifts the thousand-dollar bill, raises it for all to see. A guy in the house yells, "Don't do it!" But King doesn't hesitate. He rips it up, throwing the pieces on the platter. After a moment, he thinks out loud.

"Ah, but perhaps I've been too rash. There are so many deep, spiritual things one can do with objects of value."

He picks the pieces of broken egg off the platter. Holds them in his hands and opens his palms.

Everybody's expecting the egg to rematerialize. I guess King is too. But it doesn't. Instead, all the pieces simply fall back on the platter. A big grunt of shock from the house. King looks a little rattled. He tries scooping the pieces up again, but this time the big silver platter crashes to the floor, and all the bits of porcelain and the torn thousand-dollar bill go flying.

King's on his knees scrambling to pick up the mess. The whole crowd's whispering, trying to figure out if this is part of the act. Frankly, it looks to me like he's blowing it big.

"It seems the Buddha has a lesson to teach us all," King says. "Let go of the world, my friends, let go of the world."

And then he stands up, looks at the audience . . . and runs off.

The curtain comes crashing down, and the house lights come up. There's this stunned silence.

Needless to say, the ending was a bit of a disappointment. Everybody in the audience sits there, dazed, their mouths kind of hanging open. Then people start clearing their throats and talking to each other.

One big guy in a brown suit starts booing. About a dozen people join in, which isn't a lot, considering the size of the crowd—but they are loud.

Some people are yelling they want their money back. Others are yelling at the yellers to shut up. A no-necked bald guy shoves a no-necked booing guy who shoves him back, and pretty soon they're taking swings at each other. Ushers swarm the two no-necks, and in the confusion I scoot up to the stage and duck into the wings.

It's really dark back there, and it takes my eyes a minute to adjust. Even then, I can't really see anything but a faintly glowing line on the floor. So I follow it. And in the corner, near some ropes, I find a metal staircase. I decide to go down. This should take me to King's dressing room. I just hope Joey's otherwise occupied.

I feel my way down the metal stairs in the darkness. The edge of each step is marked with a tiny fluorescent tag. I move slowly, because I don't know how far the stairs go, and I don't much feel like somersaulting down. Finally, I hit floor. But now it's completely dark. I can't even spot the fluorescent line. I don't think I've ever been anywhere so dark. I have to blink just to be sure my eyes are open. I remember my lighter and flick on the flame, but the darkness kind of swallows the light, and I can still barely see a thing. The flame gives a bit of comfort, though, until the case heats up so much I practically burn my hand. So I pocket it again.

I stand still in the darkness. I don't know whether to go forwards or backwards. Then I think, why not go back up? I reach for the staircase, but I can't find it. I step where I think it should be, but I hit something hard, like concrete. I'm frozen there, trying to figure my next move. And starting to feel scared. Am I gonna be stuck here forever? Should I scream for help?

I reach out, trying to touch something, anything. I make contact and nearly jump out of my skin.

"Who's there?"

Silence. I'm starting to squirm. Then some arms go around me. Hands circle my neck. And a wetness. This is weird. And freaky. I'm paralyzed. Should I run? But the arms don't hurt me, they hug me. I smell a familiar smell. Reach around and feel hair. Joey.

I can't see her, but I know it's her. She's hugging me and crying.

"What happened out there tonight?" I ask.

"He's never done that before. He was already having trouble finding work. Now he'll never get a job."

"Where is he?" I ask.

"He ran off," she replies. "I don't know where."

But we both have a pretty good idea. She turns a switch and the lights come up a little. The mascara's running down her face, making her eyes look long and sad. I feel bad for her. She gets cleaned up and I walk her home.

We don't say too much the whole time we're walking. She's pretty depressed because her dad's such a mess. And I guess I'm in a lousy mood too, for exactly the same reason. Her house is pitch black. I watch her open the door with her key and ask if she's going to be okay.

"Sure," she says. "I'm just fed up with him. I'm so sick of what he does."

That makes two of us. I ask if she wants me to come in, but she's dead tired. I don't argue the point, since I'm not much in the mood either. She thanks me for being there and we kiss goodnight.

I head down the street and I'm thinking: King blew it. No payback. My stomach is burning. I'm one thousand five hundred bucks in the red, and this hole in the account, for some inexplicable reason, keeps getting bigger. It's like a pothole in winter. Fate is a mysterious and terrible thing. It doesn't give a shit about you or your problems. It's indifferent, and it eats you alive without a blink.

My brain is cooking. It's like I'm gonna spontaneously combust. I come to an abandoned lot with an old rotting fence. I stare at the fence, then I jump up, and I kick and smash and break until all of it, all forty feet of it, is just rubble on the ground.

I sit there in the moonlight getting my breath, sweat pouring off me. I stare at the moon, and I swear to you it's looking back at me. It winks. I wink back, because suddenly I feel good. Knocking down the fence was superb therapy. I released every drop of negative energy that might taint my game. The positive flow is back. I'm ready to wrestle the gods.

The next morning I get up, wash up, try to put on some jeans and a T-shirt for school. But my hands keep reaching for the sport jacket and tie. I don't want to go back to the casino. I figure I've learned my lesson on the slots for now. Let the machines cool off. Let my synapses regenerate, and pretty soon I'll be able to clean those belugas out. But I look up and there I am in the mirror, my hands tying a knot in my tie.

I go in the kitchen for a swig of milk and spot something on the table from my mom. It's her credit card bill, along with a note asking me to pay it for her at the bank machine. I barely have time to shove it in my wallet before my feet start walking me out the door, straight to the bus that will take me to the casino. I can't stay away from the place. Okay, I admit it's not just my hands and feet making me do it. My brain is, too. It's got me convinced I can get out of the hole if I just keep chipping away at it there.

I arrive soon after the doors open, feeling sharp. All my senses are in pure samurai mode. I guess that explains why, the minute I walk in, I smell something that makes me gag. Ammonia cleanser fumes waft over the scent of stale cigarettes. The whole place stinks of it. But nobody else seems to notice. They're all too busy feeding the machines. I breathe in through my nose a bunch of times to make my system adapt to the odor. It works.

I pick a slot, but the light is bad. The gas is dying in one of the neon tubes, making weird purple shadows over my hands. I look down at my feet with my samurai eyes. The carpet's got a bunch of cigarette burns in it. I scope around. The whole place looks dingy and wasted. The only thing masking the decay are the bright lights, and even some of them are burning out.

"Are you playing or what?" A short, lumpy dude in a cowboy hat is glaring at me. I blow Mr. Rodeo a kiss and start pumping away.

CHAPTER FIFTEEN

When I look up, it's Saturday. I've been working the casino almost non-stop for nearly two weeks. Part of my plan to get back the money is working. My mom hasn't seen enough of me to look me in the eye or grill me about the bankcard. My hand wrote a note on her behalf asking that I be excused from school in order to go on a family retreat in Kalamazoo. I back up my plan by scooping the bank statement and checking the phone machine for messages by remote. Six calls from Joey, two calls from Uncle Ralph, one from the school: deleted. I keep my eyes open for King, but no dice. So his bill remains outstanding.

The other part of the plan, to win back the money, is still in progress. I'm down just under seven grand.

You might think that's a lot of money. Seven Gs buys a cheap car, seven Gs buys a down payment on a condo, seven Gs buys a genius sound system. Once in a while, when I take a meal break, I watch the high rollers in action. To them, seven grand is nothing. I've seen guys blow that much on one bet. My seven grand has gone a long way, because I'm smart, and I play it slow and careful. I'm behind, but not that behind. It's just taking longer than I thought.

I'm at Horton's, nursing a coffee, flicking my lighter and calculating my potential gains from the bet I just made on the Lakers game, when somebody sits down across from me. It's Joey. She's looking pale, dark under her eyes. Needs sleep. She asks where I've been the last week.

"Working on a paper," I say. "On the ancient gods. Very demanding. I got your messages. Sorry I haven't called."

"It doesn't matter." She shrugs. Her face is like a mask.

"You don't look so hot," I say, and instantly realize what that sounds like.

"Thanks a lot." She makes like she's going to leave.

"I'm sorry, really, I'm sorry. I'm just worried about you, that's all. What's going on at home?"

"My dad's a no-show. Nobody's seen him since he walked off the stage."

Believe me, I know I haven't seen him. Wish I had.

"Oh, jeez, Joey," I say, "if I only knew what to do . . . "

"The theater manager was giving him a break. Now nobody will ever hire him again."

"That's terrible," I say and take her hand. I'm thinking my prospects to ever squeeze my money out of the welcher are getting dimmer and dimmer.

Joey's looking desperate. She says she keeps making dinners for him, hoping he'll show up for supper, like nothing's happened at all. She puts a meal on the plate and everything. And waits. She's taken to waiting till the next morning before throwing his untouched meal away. I can't believe how sad this is.

"Have you called the cops?" I ask. "Checked missing persons?"

She shakes her head. Despair. "This is a binge like I've never seen. He must be cleaned out of cash and lying low."

I tell her he's got to show up sooner or later. If he's run out of money, he'll need a place to sleep, to eat. He'll need her. Hearing that, she smiles a grim little smile.

"A repo man came today. Took the BMW. The stereo. The TV."

"Ouch."

She grips my hand. Stares at me with those riveting eyes of hers. I can see the worry pushing through her skin. It's been bad with her dad before, but this is the worst. She's never seen it like this. I feel so terrible for her, I'd do anything to make it better.

"It'll be okay," I tell her. " I'll find him."

"Where?"

"I'll check his haunts. The track, the casino, wherever. Don't worry, okay? I just don't want you to worry."

She kisses me the way no other human being on the planet can kiss. I stumble out of Horton's, reeling with her pain, determined to help her, to fix this thing, to make her happy again. I want to rip walls down, tear the planet apart to turn things around for Joey. I love her.

Then my brain gets another thought: Who's winning the basketball game?

So I scramble down the street to the Sony Store and rush in. They usually have at least twenty TVs playing. I figure one of them's got to be tuned to the game. One is, and sure enough, the Pistons are bouncing back. With a minute left, they've tied it up, and it's going back and forth. With ten seconds left, they're two up, and they're hanging on to the ball. I'm gonna get my upset. They'll win the game by two, and with the 5–1 odds I took on this one, I'll walk away with two and a half grand. Almost halfway home.

Three seconds till the buzzer and I'm smiling. But suddenly, some no-name, no-talent rookie from the Lakers steals the ball, dribbles twice and shoots from thirty feet out. Whoosh. A three-pointer. BUZZ. The game's done. The Lakers swarm their new hero, and my hole just got deeper.

Dazed, I turn to go and bump into a guy. Some kind of street cookie, because there's a real ripe smell on him. Sorry, I say. He flips around, grinning. It's King Hewitt.

"Kipper, Kip, just the man I wanted to see!"

There he is, the man I've been searching for. Why aren't I more excited to finally find him? Maybe because I can tell by his condition that paying back my money is not a big priority. But all I say is, "Joey's worried sick about you."

"I've phoned her a hundred times, Kipper, but it just rings and rings."

"Right," I say, not asking why he hasn't left a message. I get a good, long eyeful of him. He doesn't look as if he's changed his clothes in a week. His suit's dirty, frayed. There's thick stubble on his face. I get this weird thought that he'll wave his arm and be transformed into his old self. But I know it's not going to happen.

"You should go home," I tell him.

He gravely nods his head, dripping sincerity.

"I will, Kipper, believe me. But I need a hundred."

Suddenly I'm getting this ache in my stomach that isn't fictional. He wants another hundred. He put me in this mess, and the asshole wants more from me? I feel like decking him right there, smashing his head through a big-screen TV. But I show restraint.

"You already owe me six bills," I say in a quiet voice, refraining from rubbing in the fact that he promised to double it. But does he get a shamed look on his face? Does he apologize and offer to pay me back as soon as he robs a bank or something? No. The opposite. He goes on the attack.

"Owe you?" he says in a voice so loud that every single customer in the store turns to look. "*I* owe *you*?"

I'm not falling for it. I'm an expert at this ploy. I hold my ground, stare him in the face and hiss, literally hiss, the following: "Actually twelve. You said you'd double it."

I am good, but he's a pro. He gets this wounded look in his eyes. Tears start to form in the ducts. And then he winces and holds his heart to stop it from seizing up.

"You used me," he cries, "for my knowledge. For my daughter. I treated you like a son."

A gray-haired lady's been listening in. Clearly, she got used once too. She takes King's hand and squeezes five bucks into it, saying, "Ungrateful. The whole generation." Then she glares at me and hobbles off, muttering, "Scum of the earth."

She kind of takes the wind out of my sails. I decide on

another approach and try to give King a sense of what I'm going through.

"Look, I'm sorry for being rough on you, King. But try to understand, I'm pretty short myself."

He puts his arm around me, and you know, it feels good. He may smell a bit like old cheese, but it's like a big warm bear getting close to you.

"We've been through the wars together, Kipper. We both know how bad it gets in the trenches. If we don't back each other up, we'll be decimated."

That one doesn't work too well with me, seeing as I already backed him up once and got hugely stung. He gives my neck a squeeze.

"Kipper, it's my last chance. I'm this close to the big one."

I shake my head. "Aren't we all?"

Then he puts both hands on my shoulders. He gazes into my eyes. His eyes are filling up again, and tears start dripping down his face.

"I need this one, Kip. I've lost everything. I've been sleeping in alleys, in the back of cars. I can't face Joey again with my pockets empty. The girl needs her dad, doesn't she?"

I have to agree. She does. I know how rotten she's feeling. How scared she is that he hasn't come home.

"Just a hundred, please," he begs, "to placate the Goddess."

I reach into my wallet. How can I say no? But for Joey, I've got to attach one very important string. I hold the hundred-dollar bill in the air.

"On one condition: you promise to go home. Tonight."

King puts his hand over his heart.

"You have my word."

I hold out the money, and he carefully takes it from my hand. Then he kisses it.

"This is my salvation. In a few hours, Kip, I'll pay you back double."

I can't say that fills me with eager anticipation. Right now, I just want him to never borrow money from me again. And to go home to Joey.

But all I say is, "Good luck."

"We make our luck, son," he says with a smile. For the first time tonight, I see the old glint in his eye.

It's kind of hard to take, but he has nobody to blame but himself. You can just sniff it on him. The loser thing. He stinks of it. I've been taking my hits, that's for sure. But I never lose the Attitude. I know who I am. And what I can do.

CHAPTER SIXTEEN

I bus out to the Spendathon Mall hoping to bump into some of the guys. I haven't seen much of anybody lately, and I could use a little diversion to take my mind off things.

I know the Sunday Smasharama isn't on, because it's Monday, but the 3-Highs usually hang in the parking lot after hours. I am secretly praying, I must confess, that Manny is in a betting mood. Not that I'm coming to erase my deficit, but betting with him is a fun thing, a distraction. I want to get back to the old days when it was a feel-good proposition.

Sure enough, Manny is there with a few of his more formidable pals. He's very glad to see me.

"Hey, Kip, my man, come put your nose in this powder," he croons, like he's making up a song just for me. I'd sing back, but I can't carry a tune to save my life. Instead, I shake my head no to the beat. He laughs.

"You never change, Kip. Like a rock. You're the only stable dude in my stable."

I try not to think about that one too much, just chalk it up to his new powder.

"So, Manny, how're tricks? How's business?"

Manny nods a satisfied nod. "Check out my new wheels."

It's a Jag. I know this thing can't be worth less than seventy grand. He's maybe a year older than me and owns his own Jaguar. It makes me feel crazy that I'm whining about having dropped a tenth of that amount. My loss is his pin money.

"You got yourself a beautiful car there," I say.

He spits. Kicks some dirt on it.

"A beautiful piece of shit, man," he mutters. "It's a total lime."

"A lemon?" I carefully ask. "What's wrong with it?"

"Everything. The carpet's coming up, the mirror won't adjust, the heater's screwed, and more."

"Just take it in. You've got a warranty."

He hawks deep in his throat and spits a huge gob on the side of the car.

"Sure, sure, who's got time to keep going to the shop? The pig's a lime."

I get a wacky idea.

"So do the deductible," I say.

Manny lifts an amused eyebrow. His evil gang smile at the thought.

"You're a genius, Kip. This is why I like this cat. Keeps his head clear, so good ideas have a place to roost." Then he snarls at his boys: "You dumb turds should learn from him."

He turns back to me. "What's the proposition?"

I squint my eyes a little like Clint Eastwood, then peer around at the empty parking lot and the big concrete wall.

"Bet you five hundred bucks you can't total it on the wall, Manny."

My strategy is very sound. I figure he'll take it on because he won't want to lose face in front of his gang. But he's way too concerned about being a walking fashion statement to do anything that would really muss his hair. He'll try, come really close to finishing it off, but there's no way he'll follow through.

Manny laughs, sort of. More like an ear-splitting, high-pitched squeal.

"I like this bet, Kip, I like it a lot. Only I want to make two changes. You agree?"

I nod yes, wondering what kind of revisions he has in mind.

"First, we raise the stake. Two grand."

I put this worried look on my face. "Two grand?"

"Hey," Manny says, "the deductible on this dog is two. So that's what we bet. Bongo tells me you're running the high roll these days. Are you in?"

"Okay," I reply, because this is exactly what I was hoping for. I figured if I started any higher, he'd sniff a ploy.

"Second," he says, with the big smirk on his face getting bigger, "you drive."

I am, of course, taken aback by this proposal.

"That's not exactly what I had in mind," I say.

Manny gives me a grim look. His homicidal hombres look even grimmer, eyeing me like I'm destined to be their midnight snack.

"Kip, don't force me to remind you that you already agreed to my revisions. Are you reneging on me?"

"No," I say, trying to cop a plea. "It's just that I'm not much of a driver."

Manny laughs. His boys all laugh. Everybody's laughing, so I laugh a little too.

"I don't believe driving skill's a big requirement for this assignment," he says.

Juggernaut, who could have had a career as a sumo wrestler had he not become a 3-High, and Donkey, the brainless destroyer, escort me to the car. I get in, and the seatbelt wraps automatically around me. I have to admit, for a lime it's a total piece of art. Hand-carved wood paneling, velvet-soft, heated leather seats. Manny taps on the window. I hit the button and the antenna goes up. He points, and I push correctly. He smiles at me.

"Remember, Kip, you have to total it out in one shot or you lose the bet."

"Just one nagging question, Manny. The airbag. If everything else in this car is always breaking down, what about the airbag?"

"Couldn't say," Manny laughs, pinching my cheek. "Good luck."

Donkey and Juggernaut give me the thumbs-up. I rev the engine and floor it. The car stalls. They all give me the "do that again and you're dead" look. I take off the emergency brake, rev it again. It squeals off. I push the pedal to the floor and the Jag accelerates like nothing I've ever been in. I'm up to fifty and the wall is coming up fast.

Everything freezes, and in this nanosecond I contemplate my fate. Two thousand bucks. I'm gonna get two thousand bucks. I just have to sit here and let it happen. I could die for this, die because of one misguided wager. Then again, I could be about to walk away with Two Large.

My eyes open big. The wall is upon me. This is the money moment. The crunch.

But then something awful happens. My foot spasms. Suddenly, it stomps down on the brake. The Jag screeches, swerves. I try to pull my foot up, but it's locked on the pedal. I can't tear it off, and we're losing speed.

I thud forward as the car smacks the wall. My head doesn't hit the steering wheel, my neck doesn't snap backwards. Basically, I'm fine.

I stumble out of the Jag. Instantly I'm surrounded by Manny and his crew. "You're right, Manny, it's a lime. The brakes just jammed in on their own. You should get that looked at."

We inspect the damage. Manny's got this enigmatic look on his face.

"That's something, Kip. You really totaled out that fender."

I scrutinize the hood. Then I crawl under for a look. Manny and the boys lean down, peering after me.

"I may have cracked the frame," I say. "If that happened, the insurance guys'll write it off for sure."

I feel hands around my ankles. Juggernaut and Donkey pull me out from under. They scrape my back a little, but I decide not to complain. They pull me up and lean me against the car.

"This is better," I say, talking rather fast. "This way you can drive it somewhere and stage an accident so there's no hassle with the claim. This bent frame thing is a good angle, Manny, you should really have a closer look."

Manny glides up to me the way a barracuda or lamprey eel slides up to its victim.

"The only thing I'm looking at is the Two Large you now owe me."

"Double or nothing," I propose.

"No, I'm done for the night," Manny says. "Pay up."

I give him a thousand down, since I made a pre/post midnight visit to the bank machine on the way here. Juggernaut promises to find me the day after tomorrow for the second thousand. I know he will, and I know I will pay—on the dot. Not because this is fair or anything. But for one, a bet is a bet. And for two, I value the bones in my face.

I have twenty bucks left in my pocket and it's barely two a.m., so I scoot over to the casino to see if I can win some of the thousand back. I'm planning on having a bite to eat before going to the slots, but as I pass by, I see this one machine that gives me a funny twitchy feeling. It stops me cold. Is this for real? I move closer, slowly, and I can actually sense heat coming off it. I put in a couple of bucks and instantly win ten back. I have found myself a motherlode. I'm reaching in my pocket to put in some more when I feel a tap on my shoulder.

It's one of the security guards that I say hi to every day. He's got a dour look on his face.

"What's up?" I say.

"Can I see some proof of age, please?" he says.

I smile, I laugh.

"I've been coming forever, and now you want to see ID?"

"I'm sorry, there's a new manager, new policy. Just bringing us in line with the other casinos."

Taken off guard, I respond with complete lameness.

"I don't have it on me." It's the best retort I can muster. Ouch.

"Then I'm sorry, you'll have to leave."

"But this is my machine, I've been priming it, you gotta let me finish," I protest. I know it's a lost cause, and if I sound like I'm whining, it's because I am.

Without a blink, he escorts me to the doors, saying I'm welcome back as soon as I can produce proof of age. All I'm thinking is, that machine I was on was completely hot, you could feel the heat. An hour on that honey and I'd have been flush. But instead I'm screwed. And I can't come back till I get some false ID. I don't have time for that crap. I gotta move.

As I step away from the casino that just broke my heart, I notice that a crowd has gathered on the sidewalk.

I don't see an ambulance or anything, so it's not that some poor basket case collapsed at the blackjack table. Then I hear a voice and look up.

"Ladies and gentlemen: Of all the great illusions, the greatest is Life itself."

Am I really seeing this? It's King. He's standing on the flat roof of the building, about three stories up, putting on a show. He's got his magician's costume on, a top hat, all the gear. And he's in classic form, except he hasn't shaved, and his jacket's ripped at the sleeve.

"Friends," he shouts, "reality is but a sandcastle washed away by the tide, formed and reformed with each new wave. Behind it is a Greater Power pulling the strings, the Force that conceived Nature and this fragile slip of flesh."

He must have burned through my hundred in five minutes. Now he's a street performer. Do a few tricks on the rooftop and pass the hat. The crowd seems to like him.

"I was sure the Great Puppet Master had smiled on me, bestowing talent, fame and a beautiful daughter. But he turned his back, and the tide washed away the riches."

I hate to hear him blame someone else for his troubles, even if it is God. He thinks his strings are being pulled? Now that's a sure sign he's hit bottom, hard. For a minute I think I should call Joey, but I don't want to miss the performance. I figure I'll let him collect his booty after the little show, then phone her. Tag along with him till she arrives.

King puts his face in his hands for a second. He looks down at the crowd.

"And now I'm just a rock bearing down on the aching shoulders of my princess. But today, you all shall witness a miracle of nature."

He spots me. I lift my hand. He points at me and winks. Then continues.

"For I am going to alleviate my princess's burden with the most perfect feat of illusion in the repertoire of humankind."

He waves his arms in the air.

"Ladies and gentlemen: Now you see me . . . Now you don't."

And he steps off the ledge and starts to fall. Everybody gasps. One lady screams. It looks like he falls about three feet, and then there's a blast of smoke. And he's gone. The smoke clears and he's vanished into thin air. People applaud and cheer. This is totally impressive. It was great, right there in open air, no curtains, no trap doors. Must have been a bungee cord or something, but I didn't spot it. This is a stunt King can make a mint on, without gambling. He doesn't come back right away, and they clap even louder, calling for him to take a bow. One old guy's yelling, "Bravo!" And pretty soon the whole mob is chanting with him, "Bravo! Bravo! Bravo!"

They want him to reappear and pass the hat, because they want to pay, they loved the trick. But he doesn't show. He doesn't come back.

After a while people get impatient. Finally, they start to drift away. I move closer to where King was and look. There's a bit of a hidden overhang that might explain how he did the stunt. But there's no sign of King.

I stay there another half hour or so waiting to see if he's coming back. I can't help but wonder if he took off because he saw me, didn't want me hammering him for the money. But he could have collected a couple hundred easy from that crowd. It didn't make any sense. No sense at all.

CHAPTER SEVENTEEN

I wake up to the news on my clock radio. "Famed illusionist King Hewitt was found dead today, an apparent suicide." According to witnesses, he jumped off the overpass bridge on the highway at 2:30 a.m. At the same time he was doing his disappearing act. Was he in two places at once? Or did he deke the crowd and hightail it straight to the bridge?

It doesn't matter now.

I was planning to resurface at school today, but instead I skip my morning classes and head straight to Joey's house. I have to knock a couple of times before anybody answers. The door opens, and this gloomy lady with the thinnest lips of all time is standing there. She gives me a sour look.

"This isn't a good moment," she glowers, without asking who I am. But Joey appears in the doorway and tells her Aunt Lou she wants to talk to me.

We go inside, and I get a good look at Joey's face. It's puffy, red. She looks as if she's been crying for about five hours straight, which is probably accurate.

I take her hand and tell her how sorry I am, how worried I am about her.

"I had to identify the body," she says, this hollow sound in her voice. "It was my dad but it didn't look like him. His last trick: to be him but not be him at all."

At a time like this, everything that comes out of your mouth seems moronic in comparison to what the other person's going through. But I say it anyway, just because I figure I should.

"You know, what you're going through is the worst thing in the world."

"No, it's not. There are all kinds of people suffering worse than me. People sick, starving, wounded. And they're fighting to live. I can't believe he just gave up."

"Too much pressure. I guess he couldn't cope."

"No, he couldn't." She grimaces. "The idiot."

She throws herself on the couch and digs her fists into her temples. I rub her shoulders a little, trying to soothe her.

"Are you gonna be okay?"

"Yeah, sure," she says, and then her eyes take on a faraway look. "At least I don't have to deal with him any more."

"It's hard losing a father," I say.

She looks at me, her eyes flaring.

"You know what's hard? Separating the hating him from the loving him."

This completely throws me. "He was your father."

"Biologically," she snaps.

I don't get it. She sounds so cold.

"Don't you think he loved you?"

She looks at me like I have the thickest skull since Neanderthal Man. And she's probably right. The way he's treated her, it's kind of hard to expect her to really believe he loved her. If you don't treat somebody like you love them, but you tell them you love them, is that love? Saying it but not doing it? Maybe he thought he did it by killing himself for her. But it was like dropping a hand grenade on his kid's life. His troubles end; Joey's begin.

The creditors will probably take the house and everything that was left in it after the repo man's visit. Including King's collection of magicians' top hats. All they're gonna leave Joey is his clothing, and personal belongings like shaving cream. Joey has to go live with her thin-lipped aunt. So much for fatherly love. Or brotherly, the way he put me in the red.

I leave Joey to do her mourning and packing and take off. You'd think watching a guy hit bottom like that would be enough to turn me around. Well, it has. I'm completely off the slots. You won't catch me throwing away my hard-earned coin in a machine ever again. Too much is left to chance. Why go to that wanky casino and let them rip me off? Much better odds at sports. I'm gonna get out of this hole using my knowledge. I'm not gonna end up like him.

I decide to make an appearance at school, partly because I don't want to be kicked out and partly because I need to do some research. I write another note from my mom explaining that I was deathly ill with rheumatic fever, which was a possible complication from food poisoning, and I get a lot of sympathy in the office.

I head into history class and go straight to my teacher, who idolizes me even more since I explained Napoleon and Hitler's

Russian blunders to my class. I tell Ms. Kruschev about my near-death experience, and she's relieved to see me so well, though she says I still look a little pale. I explain I have a lot of catching up to do and want to fetch some statistics — research for the essay I'm writing on the nuclear arms race. She sends me to the library, saying she's eagerly awaiting my thoughts on the Cuban Missile Crisis. I make a mental note to find out what she's talking about.

In the library, I find a computer in an isolated spot and go online. I do a search for the latest statistics on sports. I want up-to-date scores, the scoop on the teams and info about the injured lists. I used to fetch these stats to win little bets with Bongo. Now thinking about those times makes me a bit blue. There was nothing to it then, betting a buck here, a quarter there. Win or lose, it was all for a laugh. The good old days.

Within a couple of minutes I get the lowdown on everybody in the playoffs. Moss broke his wrist. Greenblatt is back, but his concussion's still bothering him. For sure the Blackhawks are going to win tomorrow. And the Stars and the Avalanche and — I've got everything I need at my fingertips. Knowledge is power, and with this kind of information, the power is mine.

I'm about to leave the computer when I notice a site on the browser. ON LINE SPORTS. Curious cat that I am, I click, and lo and behold. It's a casino on the Net, located in the scenic Netherlands. It's stunning, really. Here I am, in the grotty hell-hole of Louis Pasteur High School, and with a flick of my pinky, I'm high-rolling it in Amsterdam. I feel like Scottie finally beamed me up.

It's all there, every game, every sport. You can bet on the point spread or the total points—over or under. I get a sinking feeling when I realize it takes a credit card to log on, and I don't have one. Then I'm comforted by the realization that I have the next best thing. I neglected to pay my mom's charge card bill, and it's still safe in my wallet. I pull it out, key in the card number and set up an account. With the money she owes, there's only a couple of grand left on her credit limit, but that should do. The machine says no one under eighteen can legally play, but since the account's in my mom's name, and she's forty, everything is cool. No security guard to bust me in cyberspace. And get this: the maximum win they allow in one day is thirty thousand dollars. I figure I can live with that.

I place my bets. Fifty that the Bucks win by ten. A hundred that the Raptors lose by eight. Seventy-five bucks says the Leafs score the first goal. Two hundred, the Blackhawks win by two. And so on.

I can't believe how lucky I am. I found the Web casino in the nick of time. It's a gimme, a no-brainer. The big money's there, you just have to take it. King didn't know when to quit. He kept going after he lost his nerve. Not me. Once I've got a big enough stake, I'm done. All I want to do is to double my university fund, so I've got a start once I get my BA. No stars in these eyes. I'm not looking for a million. Just a modest, achievable goal.

I put three hundred on Dallas winning by three and call it a day. I'll know by tomorrow night how much I've cleaned up.

God, I love computers.

CHAPTER EIGHTEEN

Wednesday night, I pop into the Sony Store to catch the final scores. The first one is good news; I called the Leafs spot on. That put me seventy-five up. The rest of the news is making my gut start to burn, however. I'm close, very close, but unfortunately, they don't pay out on close. I have taken a major beating. But all is not lost. After I pay off the charge card bill I'll still have a bit of a stake left in the bank and other options to be considered. These thoughts are interrupted by a terrible odor that's roasting my nostrils. I look over my shoulder to see a vision from Hell: Donkey and Juggernaut.

"Manny was asking about your health," Juggernaut sniggers.

"Urng," agrees Donkey.

"Tell him I'm feeling terrific," I say to them, though I'm not being completely honest. Then again, I don't think they really care.

They move a little closer. They each put a huge hand on one of my shoulders.

"I love you too, guys," I say, "but that doesn't mean I go both ways, if you get my point."

They don't. And if they squeeze any harder they'll be crushing bone.

"I'm ready to pay." I wince, the pain blistering down my arms. "Let's hit the machine."

"Ungh," Donkey says, glad to hear my suggestion.

As we walk to the bank machine, I try to discuss some of the larger issues with them.

"It's depressing, really, the negative effect bad Hollywood action films have had on the youth of today. You guys should be playing football, not pretending to be thugs in a Jackie Chan movie."

Unfortunately, Juggernaut misses the irony and backhands me.

We arrive at the machine, and I take out five hundred.

"That's only five," says Juggernaut, stating the obvious.

"There's a five-hundred daily maximum," I reply. "I explained that to Manny."

"He wants it all now," Juggernaut says and punches me in the stomach. I buckle over. For a minute I can't breathe. My gut was already in dicey shape, and this love tap doesn't help. Donkey pulls me up and Juggernaut smacks me across the face. I can taste blood in my mouth.

"I don't like the flavor," I tell them, perhaps unwisely, because Donkey gives me a kick in the crotch. Somehow he misses the family jewels, but I still see a flash of light and hit the pavement hard.

Juggernaut leans over and squeezes my throat.

"We'll be here at 12:01. Is it a date?"

"Uh huh," I gasp.

They leave, and I get up very slowly, checking to see how bad the damage is. My stomach's kind of throbbing, but I'll live. I'm mostly just bruised, and the cut inside my mouth will heal pretty fast. Mouth cuts do. I'll just have to back off the OJ for a few days.

I hobble into a gas station and grab the key to the washroom. When I get inside, I look in the mirror and check myself out. I don't look good. Pale, depressed. No obvious wounds on my face, however. My cheek's a little puffy, but nothing major. Probably no internal damage, though the aching in my gut won't quit. I go into a stall and drop my pants for further inspection. It's pretty red where Donkey kicked me. And it's starting to swell.

I splash some water on my face and consider my situation.

At this point I am not exactly flush. And, without much of a stake, I'm not going to have a chance to get back ahead.

I need to pick up some fast bucks. How? There's got to be a way out of this.

Then it hits me. Uncle Ralph. On a good night waiting tables, I can take home a hundred bucks with tips. That's all I need to turn this thing around.

My mood improves enormously. I head over to the Golden Goose, limping only slightly. I check myself in the glass before heading in. I look okay. Better than okay. I'm ready to work. I walk in the door, nod to the waiter who's serving a table. He looks pretty green. I head past him into the kitchen.

Uncle Ralph's pulling the gizzard out of a chicken. I slip

into the narrow space across the cutting table from him and raise my hand hello. He gets this pained look on his face.

"Ooph! Kippy, what are you doing to me?"

I can tell he's a little peeved.

"For the last two months I'm covering for you, ooph! Cutting you slack just 'cause you're my nephew. What do you think I am?"

He's definitely in a bad mood. I have to raise the emotional stakes to get him onside, that's for sure. I go all hangdog and give him a totally pathetic look. Which isn't hard to manage, because I'm pretty close to 100 percent pathetic right now anyway. I press the sore spot on my leg and moan. He squints at me.

"You hurting?"

"My leg, it's damaged."

"See a doctor. What else?"

"The truth is, my girlfriend's dad killed himself. She's in real rough shape."

"That's too bad. I wish I gave a crap."

Oh man, he is not going to be an easy sell. I decide to pull out all the stops.

"Remember how you helped my mom and me when my dad died? I'm just trying to help her out, Uncle Ralph. Like you did."

He doesn't blink.

"Good, Kippy. You keep helping her out. You've got lots of time now."

I can't believe this. Even my trump card isn't enough.

"But Uncle Ralph . . ."

"First I call, I leave you messages. No reply."

I'm scrambling now. I'm straining.

"C'mon, Uncle Ralph, the machine's on the fritz . . . "

"I stopped calling, 'cause your ma answers the phone. I can't keep asking her where you are, it'd break the poor woman's heart."

I guess I should be grateful for that. She would've been scared to death about me. Then Uncle Ralph yanks the last bit of intestine out of the dead chicken and throws it in the sink.

"You didn't leave me any choice, Kippy. I had to hire somebody else. Find another job, and I'll give you a glowing recommendation."

He goes to the sink and scrubs his hands.

"You got your start from me, Kip. I gave you the help to get you to university. I'm totally square with your father, may he rest in peace. Now we're finished, and my hands are clean. See you at Christmas dinner."

And he walks back into the dining area, leaving me there with the pulled-out chicken guts. I limp out the service exit.

I'm at the bank machine at midnight and dutifully pay Manny's minions the last of the cash. Juggernaut takes the five hundred and punches me in the stomach. Donkey smacks me across the ear.

"What was that for?" I ask.

"You owe interest," Juggernaut replies and pulls me into the alley.

"For what? I paid you fast," I say, my ear still ringing from the smack.

"Not fast enough," says the Jug. Donkey throws me into a bunch of garbage cans.

"Wait, wait!" I beg him. "You don't understand. I gave you the last of my cash."

Juggernaut puts his face so close to mine, I can smell the nachos on his breath. He smiles, his chipped front tooth glinting like a fang six inches from my nose. "So what else do you got?"

I dig into my pockets, and I touch it. My dad's lighter. For a second I feel my dad's fingers on the metal. I grip it the way he gripped it.

"All I got is some change," I say.

"You're holding back on us. Turn him over, Donkey."

Donkey, clenching and unclenching his hands like a bad sci-fi alien, moves in. In a flash, he grabs both my wrists. I keep my fists closed tight. Donkey pulls them to the ground.

"You open 'em or he opens 'em."

Since there's nothing in my left hand, I open it.

"The other one."

"It's just change."

Jug nods to Donkey, who puts his boot on my fist. Pieces of gravel cut through the skin on the back of my hand. He puts more pressure on, and the bones in my fingers start to give.

"Okay," I say. "You can have it."

Donkey lifts his foot and opens my hand.

Juggernaut snatches the lighter. "Looks good. What's it worth?"

"Nothing much," I tell him. "It just has sentimental value."

"Bullshit." He laughs, punches me in the stomach again and walks off with it. Donkey follows, and Jug flares it in his nose. They leave, making sparks and chuckling.

Go ahead, I think, take the lighter. I hope it burns a hole in your leg. I hope a stray spark gets in your eye and makes you go blind. I hope you swallow it by mistake and choke to death.

I don't know why I'm getting upset, why I'm practically crying. I've got no use for the lighter anyway. I don't smoke, I don't make forest fires, what the hell do I need it for? The stupid thing was just taking up room in my pocket. Wearing holes in the fabric. Wearing holes in me. I'm better off without it. Way better off.

Not having any other compelling prospects, I head home. Think maybe I'll stand in the shower for a couple of hours, reconnect my synapses. I stick the key in the lock and step in quietly, figuring my mom's probably asleep, which is a good thing.

But she's not. In fact, she's on her way to work. She's had a schedule change, and she's totally pumped that I'm home before she has to go. I stick my scraped hand in my pocket and say hello. She's got this smile on her face and is waving a big brown envelope.

"Kip, Kip, it's from the university!"

"Oh, yeah?" I say, not exactly oozing excitement.

"I've been waiting all day for you to open it!"

So I do. And I get a paper cut doing it. The letter is pretty straight ahead:

Dear Kipling Breaker,

This is to inform you that you have been accepted for entrance to our university's fall semester. We hope that blah, blah, blah, blah, blah, blah, blah, blah, blah, blah . . .

Sincerely,
Adrian Stickuphisass
Director of Admissions

The rest of the thing spells out the dates and times for registration, with all kinds of forms and crap that I'm supposed to fill out. Mom's over the moon.

"Kip, you got in! Congratulations!"

"Thanks," I reply, not really sharing her enthusiasm.

"Aren't you excited? It's incredible! Your daddy would be so proud!"

"Maybe."

"What are you talking about? You'll have an education, something neither of us ever had. Why aren't you happy?"

Fact is, the whole thing depresses the hell out of me, and you know why. But she looks at me, studies my face with those deep eyes of hers.

"Is something going on, Kip?" she asks me, really gently, really sweetly. My mom can be so nice sometimes. I want to just spill, you know, tell her the whole thing. And I almost do, I almost feel my mouth start to sob the whole thing out. But it'd kill her. I can't do that.

So I tell her the part of the truth I think she can handle.

"I'm just really, really disappointed they didn't offer me a scholarship. I feel like a failure."

She smiles and strokes my head. "The last thing in the world you are is a failure. You're pure success, Kip. Besides, you could try the scholarship exams, and you have your savings."

"Sure, I know," I shrug. "It's just not the same."

Then, innocent that she is, she comes up with a perfectly generous idea.

"If you're worried about the whole four years, Kip, we should just start putting more money in."

"No, Mom, that's okay, really," I say quickly, trying to squash that idea and her next logical thought. I fail.

I can see the thought configure in her head: her eyes get cloudy, her forehead creases, she licks her lips, and then she says the two words I've been dreading for weeks.

"The bankcard."

Throughout history, when confronted with two words, people have reacted in different ways. WE SURRENDER are two words that have stopped wars and saved millions of lives. NOT GUILTY has given thousands of innocent people freedom. PLAY BALL has started a trillion baseball games and given countless fans joy. But THE BANKCARD has no positive spin for me. THE BANKCARD. Two words that will crumble my life into nothingness.

This entire thought process flashes through my brain as the two words slip out of her lips. Some other combinations of two words also zip through my consciousness, such as

DEAD DUCK, LAME LOSER, STUPID WANKER, and so on.

I do not, however, reveal any of the above to my mother. Instead, I put on my most innocent, busy-student persona and say, rather distractedly, "Oh, it's in my room. Do you want it now?"

"No problem, darling. I appreciate you taking care of the banking for me the last while, but it's really my responsibility. Just give it to me when you have a chance."

"Sure thing," I say, and watch her start to exit for her late shift. Quick thought has once again bought me a little time. I exhale relief. But then, instead of going out the door, my mom turns back and looks at me.

"Kip."

My gut flutters as if it's filled with moths cremating themselves on the candle that's burning a hole in my stomach lining.

"Yeah, Mom?" I reply, trying to sound calm.

"Tell me you're happy."

"I am, Mom. I'm thrilled. I truly am."

She smiles. Light's jumping off her face. Her dream for me has finally come through.

"I am so proud of you, kid."

She blows me a kiss and steps out. The door clicks shut. I lean against the wood and lock it. How am I supposed to tell her there is no college fund? Dallas lost, and that will eat the last of it. I don't expect her to understand. If she saw the bank balance right now, even before I pay off the credit card, she'd have a coronary. A stroke. A coronary and a stroke.

I strip and go into the shower. The water's as hot as I can

take it. This isn't a masochistic thing, I'm not into getting blisters or anything. I just need to boil my brains out for an hour.

The heat feels good on my sore spots, and the steam vaporizes my mind. It doesn't take long for the Attitude to resurrect itself. Because it's not a big deal, really. It's just Twelve Large. Guys flush that much down the toilet at the tables every minute. And I'm the guy who turned twenty-five cents into nearly three hundred bucks. At the track, three hundred bills at 20–1 makes six big ones. Turn that around a few more times, and I've got four years of university paid for and nobody'll know the difference.

I just need a little stake.

CHAPTER NINETEEN

I go to school feeling subdued. I kind of sleepwalk through my classes, just putting in the time while I recharge my batteries. Everybody else has heard from the U or other schools too, and all they're blabbing about is where they're gonna live, who they're gonna live with and the classes they're gonna take. Unless they're the ones who didn't get in. You can spot them a mile away, licking their wounds in the dark corners. If I could projectile vomit on cue, I'd be a force to contend with, believe me.

When school's over, I'm still trying to formulate a plan when the plan comes to me. Bongo.

"Hey, Kip. Kipperino!"

I smile at the sight of my deliverance.

"Hey, Bong-man, what's doing?"

"I'm like flush, Kipster, I just scored two hundred bucks on the Pro Select. Dallas folded, everybody knew they would. How much did you win on that game, man?"

Internally, I wince. "Everybody knew they would?" Where'd he hear that? I sussed the stats, I read up on what was going. What did I miss? But I don't reveal any of this internal angst to him. I just give him a sly smile.

"Plenty," is all I say, and he of course buys it.

"The Kipster! He plays it close, never tips his hand, always keeps the Attitude."

"Looks like you're doing good," I say.

It's true. Apart from the chocolate smeared on the creases of his lips, and the breadcrumbs on his shirt, Bongo is looking very healthy and prosperous. This is confirmed when he flashes a roll of bills at me.

"Not your way, Kip, I'm just in it for fun. I wish I could be like you: serious, a pro, total balls. I'm just nickel and dime—you, you are It, man!"

It's an amazing thing how the mythology that surrounds you can completely blind people to what's really going on inside. But after all, that's the basic premise of a game like poker. Never show your hand.

"So, Bong, spot me a fifty, spare me a hike to the machine."

Bongo grins. He's eating this up.

"No way. You have to win it."

He pulls a fifty out of his roll and holds it up in the air.

"Three chances to guess the last digit of the serial number."

"I like the odds," I say.

"Anything for a friend. So what is it?"

A month ago I would've walked away from him. Who's he think he is, doing this to my face? Making me guess numbers instead of just handing me the cash. But he doesn't know I'm strapped. To him, it's just a game. So I play.

My first guess is Two. And I'm wrong. So I guess again.

"Seven."

"Nay."

Before I use my last chance, I close my eyes, concentrate, try to visualize what's on the bill. And something incredible happens. I start to buzz and tremble. I feel myself fill up with light. Then my spirit lifts out of my body, floats over both of us. I can see myself standing there with Bongo, my eyes still closed. I float behind him and look over his shoulder. And I see the number. I see it! Instantly my spirit's back in my body. I open my eyes and say it.

"Five."

Bongo gets this stunned look on his face and shakes his head. Smiles and shows me the bill.

"No, it was three. I thought for sure you'd get it. Guess you're hoofing it to the bank."

Chortling, he turns his back and goes.

It doesn't make sense. What's wrong with me, mistaking a three for a five? I astral project for the first time in my life and go myopic? Maybe I'm losing it, maybe the stress is just freaking out my brain.

I go to the park, figuring if I stare at the ducks for a while things will start to make sense. I don't have anything to feed them, but there's an empty bag with a half-eaten sandwich in it. I consider eating it myself but think better of sharing a stranger's saliva.

I'm throwing crumbs at my little quacking friends when I feel hands cover my eyes. For a second I think it's Juggernaut and they've decided to beat me up again, but I smell a fragrant scent. It's Joey. She looks so fine. I pull her down beside me.

"Feels like a year since I saw you last," she says.

"Yeah," I say, "every minute's like an hour."

She smiles. I love looking at her face. I am one very happy person to see her. I don't even ask how she found me. I don't care. I'm just glad she's here.

"Sorry for not calling. Things have been heating up everywhere."

"I've been pretty tied up too," she says, "between the move and all the legal crap with the will and everything."

"How are things with your aunt?"

"She's been really great," Joey says, her eyes getting a little watery. "If she wasn't around, I don't know what I'd do."

"You'd have me to take care of you," I smile.

"That's a terrifying thought," she replies and kisses me. "My aunt was wondering if you wanted to come for dinner tomorrow."

"Dinner? Yeah, sure, why not?" I say. "I can be off then."

She tilts her head a little, checking me out. This could be dangerous.

"You don't seem very excited to see me."

I instantly perk up. "Are you kidding? I'm just a little preoccupied, that's all."

Now her feelers are really up. She doesn't even have to ask me why. I'm obligated to explain.

"My courses next year," I lie. "I can't decide what to take."

She shakes her head. I can't tell if she's buying it or not. "But school's months away. I haven't even decided which school I'm going to yet."

"I mean the future, you know? Like my major."

She stares at me. "You don't pick that till your second or third year."

"Guess I have ants in my pants."

I'm not sure if she buys it. She looks at the pond. Thinking.

"I've seen that look before."

"Where?" I ask, trying to figure out whether I've actually screwed up or if this is just part of the trauma thing from losing her dad.

"Forget it," she says, and I am somewhat relieved. "So are you coming?"

"For dinner? Absolutely."

She wants to call her aunt right away, and there's a phone just by the washrooms on the other side. She asks me to watch her pack for her while she dashes over.

When she's out of sight, I try to stay focused on the ducks, but my eyes keep moving over to her pack. I notice the zipper isn't closed completely, and that isn't good. I reach over to zip it closed, but something strange happens. My hand slips into the pack. I try to will it out, but it won't obey. So I yank on it with my other hand and the unruly mitt emerges, but it's holding something. Her wallet.

All of a sudden both my hands are going wild. I can't stop them. They're like piranhas, attacking her wallet, tearing through her cash. She's got sixty bucks in there. One hand pulls out a twenty. I try to replace the bill but the other hand has already stuck it in my pocket and I'm rushing to get the wallet back in the pack, so it's too late to return the money.

I tell myself this is beyond my control. Couldn't be helped. Besides, she loves me, I love her, and it's strictly a loan. I'll get the money back to her before she notices.

But then I look up. Joey's staring at me with this strange expression on her face.

"I had a feeling, but I didn't want to trust it."

"What are you talking about?"

She keeps gazing at me like she's a microscope and I'm bacteria.

"Your vanishing act. Your not calling. Your excuses."

"I'm busy, that's all," I stammer.

"When you said you'd find my dad, you were so sure of yourself. Knew just where to look."

"You told me he gambled. I was guessing."

"You were with him, weren't you?"

I feel frozen inside. But I still play dumb. Deny, deny. She's on me, though. She witnessed what I did, and now she knows all. She's put it together. She saw the way I connected with her dad.

"You did the track with him, didn't you?"

I try to shake my head no, but I'm not very convincing.

"What about the casino?"

All I can do is shrug under her cold, analytical gaze. I don't like this feeling, it's like we're a million miles apart. I try to take her hand, but she pulls away. And tells me what really spilled it for her.

"It was that look on your face . . . just like him."

I beg her to let me explain, let me try to make it right, but she just stares at me.

"I fell so hard for you. I loved your edge, your jokes, your dreams. That's what caught me: you were just like him."

"I'm not, Joey, you gotta believe me."

"I always wanted to believe him too. I can't do that any more."

I plead with her not to give up on me, because I really do want to fix this thing. I want it to be better between us.

"Joey, don't get me wrong. I'm with you, okay? I'll sort this thing out and everything'll be cool, I promise. I'm gonna get that boat for us, I really am. We'll sail across the Pacific, head straight to New Guinea."

She's like ice, but I keep trying. "Remember? We'll lie on our backs on the deck, just you and me, watch a million billion stars in the sky." Then I look up. Like an omen, a good blessing, I see it shining. "Look, a star. First one in the sky. That star's for us."

She squints her eyes at it. Then shrugs. "That's no star, it's just a satellite. Space junk."

I laugh, my heart sinking. "Joey, give me one more chance. Please. I love you."

Her face softens. I know she heard me, because she loves me too. She gazes at me with those beautiful black eyes. Then she holds out her hand.

"Give me back my money."

I go to say something else, but she just glares at me. I'm biting my lower lip so hard I think it's gonna bleed. She doesn't budge. I pull out the twenty and hand it to her, saying, "I was gonna pay you back tomorrow. No lie."

But that's not the kind of line that really works with the daughter of a dead compulsive gambler, I guess. She's probably heard it every day of her life. She looks at the twenty and shakes her head. I'm surprised to detect a touch of sympathy in her face.

"You must be pretty desperate to have lifted this from me."

I'm relieved. She understands—and she's holding the bill out, it's almost there for me to take.

"I've just gotta get out of the hole, Joey. It won't take long. I know I can do it if you're with me. It's you and me, right? Together we can do anything."

A tiny little smile crosses her lips, and she pulls the bill out of my grasp. "Here's a trick you'll appreciate."

Joey pulls out a wooden match, flicks it with her nail, and there's a flame. Takes the twenty and torches it. I try to grab it from her, but she shoves me away. She drops it before it burns her fingers, and I dive for it, but all that's left is ash. Then I remember. It's magic. A trick.

"Very funny," I say. "Bring it back, okay?"

She shakes her head. "Sorry, I can't."

I'm starting to get irritable. "Sure you can, where'd you palm it?"

But she just picks up her pack, throws it over her shoulder and eyeballs me.

"Come on, Kip," she says. "You know this trick. You do it all the time."

When I first met her, I thought she staggered me. I didn't know what staggered meant until now.

"You really burned it?" I ask, because I can't believe it's true. But it is. She cremated it. "Are you insane?" I scream at her. "What the hell's wrong with you?" But she doesn't look crazy at all. She's got tears pouring out of her eyes. I go to hold her, but she backs off. Then she turns and walks away, leaving me with the ducks and a pile of ashes.

I should be upset, but instead I'm feeling kind of numb, sitting here studying what's left of the twenty. There is one little corner that survived. I'm wondering, if I take the corner and the ashes to the bank, will they exchange it for the real thing? They could chemical test it or something to prove it's really a twenty. Actually, why not tell them it was a fifty? How would they know the difference?

But then I feel something wet on my head. A drop of rain. I start scooping up the ashes, but suddenly it's Noah's ark time, and it all washes away. No big deal, I guess. I'd probably have to wait a couple days for them to test and process it—and I don't have that kind of time.

Then I get an excellent, life-saving idea. Go home. Pick up my stereo and camera. They're worth at least a couple of hundred at the pawnshop. I'll find one of those twenty-four-hour places and score the cash. This is inspired. This is an answer. This is a stake I can combine with the one asset nobody can take away from me: the Thing. The Special. It makes me unstoppable. I maintain the winning attitude because I'm still having fun. The fun is key. That's what keeps it special. And I've got it. I am having fun.

I go up the walk of our duplex, trying for the life of me to remember if Mom's working tonight. I can't exactly recall what her work nights are since she got rescheduled. Which wouldn't actually help, because I'm not absolutely sure what day today is. It's been a long one, you know what I mean?

It seems too risky just to walk in. I don't want her to catch me hocking my last two birthday presents. If she's there, I'll wait her out. Let her go to sleep, and then I'll do the deed. So I start checking the windows to see if anybody's home. Living room's clear. I go around the corner and flatten myself against the kitchen window.

I stay close to the brick and lean in very slowly. Coast is clear. She must be sleeping upstairs. I open the door. Very quietly. Slip off my shoes. Gently padding down the hallway, I pass the kitchen. Maybe I'll nip in and do a fast face-stuff.

As I reach for the fridge door, I notice the mail's on the table. Only one letter's open. I look more closely.

It's the bank statement. All the withdrawals I've made are circled in red.

My stomach goes limp and turns over. I hold onto a chair, because all of a sudden I'm feeling woozy. And then I hear her voice, calling from upstairs: "Kip? Is that you? We have to talk."

I bolt. I grab my shoes and push out the door. Run around to the side and dive into the bushes. Put on my shoes and just lie there in the dirt trying to decide what to do. How can I face her? How could I ever face her again?

All I can do is try and make it right. I have to get the money back.

I figure I'll head downtown and just ask around, see if anybody there's feeling flush enough to help me turn a one-eighty.

The streetlamp's dead on this corner, but there's an awning out of the rain, a good thing since it's getting chilly. I stand there in the half-light looking for a benefactor. I ask the first couple of people who pass by for a little donation, but they just walk faster. A few more cross the street to avoid me.

Okay, I'm cold, I'm shaking a bit, and the rain's got me appearing a little soaked. And yeah, some of that ash got on my clothes. But my intentions are good. Under normal circumstances, I'm quite a presentable guy. Some would even say I'm buff. Everybody should just relax. You've got nothing to fear from me. Promise.

I guess I'm standing there, getting colder and hungrier, for another couple of minutes—or is it hours? It feels like forever.

I'm almost falling over from the whole thing when I see an older guy strolling my way. He's got a big-brimmed hat and a long overcoat on, and a silk scarf wrapped around his face. He's all in black, a fairly cool look that would require major coin to acquire.

Something about this guy makes me feel I've found my man. It's him. I know it. Timing's everything. Not too soon, not too late. I have to wait till he's two feet away, no more, no less. Have to be able to feel his energy, and have him feel mine. I wait, wait, wait. Now.

"Hey, mister, how about a little wager?"

He stops dead. Bingo. He doesn't say anything. Between his hat and his scarf, just his eyes are showing. They keep gazing at me.

"Just flip a quarter. You call it in the air. What do you say? This isn't a panhandle, it's an honest bet."

He keeps staring at me, but he doesn't say anything, so I push harder. I don't want to, but I can't help it. I'm cold, that's all. I'm tired. I admit what I say sounds lame, but I can't stop the words.

"Please, mister, I need this. I really need this," I say, hating myself for sounding like such a loser. But it's my last shot, what can I do? If I scare him off, so be it.

He doesn't walk away. He keeps standing there. I wish I could see his face. But then he says something.

"I like to bet."

"Good, good, that's great. Do you have a quarter? I don't have any small change, you see." I'm thinking even a quarter's a start. A quarter once gave me three hundred bucks, did I tell you that?

He reaches into his pocket and pulls out a brand new, sparkling quarter. I think it's the most beautiful coin I've ever seen in my life.

"You're great, man, you're wonderful, you're a prince," I say, and I mean it. I'm so happy this guy stopped to flip with me. But then he says something that sends chills so big down my skin that I stop shaking from the cold.

"No, I'm the King," the guy says, and he takes off his scarf.

It's him. The King. King Hewitt. He smiles at me.

"How are you, Kipper?"

I'm so stunned I can barely get the words out. All I can do is stammer. "But you're . . . you're . . . "

He laughs. The same old laugh that would shake up a room. He looks great, better than ever.

"There's no escape from it, Kip. I thought death would be the end of my travails, but it seems there's no way out. I'm precisely where I left off: behind."

It sounds like being awake in a nightmare, I think to myself. He may look good, but now he's a perpetual bottom feeder.

"Precisely. My curse is to be chasing it forever."

I'm floored. He can read my mind.

"A small comfort," he continues. "For I'm alone, forsaken by the gods, lost to the one person I truly loved."

I lost her too. I think about how Joey looked at me before she turned her back. I don't blame her. Who could?

"It's never too late, son."

He's right in my head. It's unsettling, it truly is, not having to speak because he's reading my thoughts like a newspaper.

"What if I could undo it all, Kip? Replace your twelve thousand in the bank. Get you on your feet so you could face your family, win back the princess and start university in the fall?"

It's a joke, right? This can't really be an offer. But he came back from the dead. Maybe he *is* a master of time and space. Could he reverse everything that's happened, just rewind me and let me do it all over again?

"Son, nothing would make me happier," he smiles. "Flip you for it."

Flip me? How do you flip for something like that? For your whole life? King chuckles at my thought. With every laugh, he flickers. Sometimes I can see right through him.

"Win, Kip, and all your riches will be restored to you. You'll be back in the fat. Lose, and you join me. For all eternity. Of course, you could also choose not to bet. But there are no odds in that, are there?"

He puts his arm around me, the way he used to, the old bear arm. It warms me right up. For a dead guy, his arm feels really soft and comfortable.

"So, my old comrade-in-arms, what will it be: heads or tails? It's your call."

I'm trying to speak, but my mouth won't move. I want to say tails, but I can't get my lips to cooperate. My tongue is numb, my teeth won't open. I grab my mouth with my hands, but my jaw muscle has turned to rock. All I have to do is say one word, but my mouth is shut tight. It won't let me call it. I can't make the call.

King starts laughing. Louder and louder, until my ears are splitting. I can't take the sound, it's making my whole body shake and spin and the sidewalk turns into a whirlpool and it's sucking me in and I'm fighting it but I can't hold on, I'm going down, going down, down.

There's an intense light in my eyes. Could this be It? The White Light? I've finished the game, and now I have to take that last flight to the Other Side. I open my eyes. The light is so bright, it's blinding. I hear a voice far away in the distance.

I look at the angels, or devils, or whatever it is come to get me. There are two of them. A blue aura emanates from their garments.

I squint to pull them into focus.

"You got some ID, kid?"

They are cops.

They ask me two million questions. While I'm telling them some crap, they get called on a robbery, so they let me go and squeal away, siren blaring. I watch the red lights spin until they turn a corner and disappear.

I start walking. My idea is . . . no idea. My plan is . . . no plan. I'm down to zero. Nothing. Nothing in my pockets, nothing in the bank, nothing in my stomach.

I can still walk. I watch my feet on the concrete, one step after the other. I'm moving. I'm watching myself moving. It's interesting, isn't it, how you can do that. Each step taking you somewhere. I'm not falling down. That's something. That truly is something. A start.

CHAPTER TWENTY

My new weekend job is great, better than great. On a good week I can walk away with two hundred bucks in commissions. If you need a good deal on a car stereo, talk to me. I can set you up with something that will make your ears bleed.

Most nights I'm bussing tables at the Sea Star Café, which is, as you know, the top seafood place in town. The *New York Times* critic walked in last month and raved, so now people can't get a reservation. But if you want to check out the black risotto, let me know, I'm pals with the maitre d'. I can even get you a free drink. I share the tips with the waitresses, so this job is actually top of the line.

With these two gigs and the weekday bathroom-cleaning job, I'll pull in enough cash by the end of the summer to cover the first semester of school anyway. At least, that's the bet I'm making with myself.

That's the only kind of bet I'm making these days. The other kind is for losers. From now on, the only non-fiction bets I make are gonna be with other people's money.

I can't believe it took me this long to sort it out. It was one of those beautiful flukes. A few days after hallucinating King, I was trying to figure my next move when I felt this lump in my pocket. It was his newspaper obituary. I flipped it over, and there's a column of little numbers. I wondered if it was some kind of message from beyond. I stared at it, trying to decipher all the figures. Then it hit me. It's the Dow-Jones averages. I'm looking at all those little numbers and thinking, each number is money. Each number is a lot of money. How do I get some?

So I make a plan: Do a degree in business, make some connections, get out and become a stockbroker. These guys have it made. Why put your own cash on the line when people will actually pay you to lose theirs for them? King was totally nickel-and-dime compared to this. The stock market isn't just legal gambling, it powers the whole economy. I get to be rich and be a patriot all at the same time. You gotta love this. Total win-win-win.

I'm pretty sure my mom's still trying to get over what happened. She's been sleeping with her wallet under her pillow ever since she found out. Someday I think she'll trust me again. Might take a while, though. Anyway, in a few years I'll be making it all straight with her. Make her proud again. I'll set her up like royalty. Like a queen. I mean it.

Every so often, I used to go ring on Joey's aunt's door. Nobody ever answered, though I'm pretty sure somebody was home. Then, the last time I went there, her aunt opened the door. Told me Joey had gone away to school. I asked for her address. She just closed the door.

It doesn't bother me that Joey doesn't want me around.

Nothing bothers me. I can't let it. Do that, and you lose the Thing. You lose it all. I just look forward. Because I know that one day I'll find her again. I will. And it doesn't stop there. You see, I made a bet with myself. Two hundred that I get her back. Even odds.